THE 9TH DIRECTIVE

Adam Hall is recognized as one of today's foremost spy writers. His first novel *The Berlin Memorandum* was an instant success, (it went on to film and paperback fame as *The Quiller Memorandum*), and was followed by seven more 'Quiller' novels which have all been best-sellers.

In real life Adam Hall is Elleston Trevor, author of several highly successful adventure stories including *The Flight of the Phoenix*; he also writes novels as Howard North and serious historical treatises as Roger Fitzalan.

An Englishman, Adam Hall lived for many years in the South of France and since 1973, in Arizona, U.S.A.

ADAM HALL

The 9th Directive

FONTANA/Collins
By agreement with William Heinemann Ltd

First published by William Heinemann Ltd 1966
First issued in Fontana Paperbacks 1975
Sixth impression January 1987

Copyright © Adam Hall 1966

Made and printed in Great Britain by
William Collins Sons & Co. Ltd, Glasgow

CONTENTS

Chapter One

THE BLOODSTONE

The place was half-way along Soi Suek 3 and I walked there from the main road where the trishaw had dropped me. It was a narrow street of shop-houses, roofed at this moment by the twilight.

There was no one in the gem-shop except the small old Thai at the work-bench behind the counter; he did not hear me come in because of the noise of the gem-tumbler that churned at the back of the shop. There was no air-conditioner and the heat was as bad as in the street. From a room above came the weird notes of a *pi-nai*.

I stood watching the old man. He was making a ring, setting an opal in gold. It was a *cabochon* stone and the blade of his burnisher closed the claws of the bezel so deftly that they seemed hinged. The light of the hooded lamp reflected the gold and struck fire in the gem. When the last claw was pressed home he turned to look at his work under the lamp and saw me. I said at once: 'Mr Varaphan?'

He put the ring down on to the black cloth and made me the *wai* greeting with his hands, gently as a priest.

I asked: 'Is the bloodstone ready?'

'It has been lost,' he said.

'But it was worth more than a million pounds.'

'Much more, yes.'

'Then you must pay me.'

'I am a poor man,' he said. 'You cannot get blood out of a stone, even a bloodstone.'

'Then give me my pound of flesh.'

He bowed slightly in passing me and went to the open door-way, watching the street, his head turning from left to right. I waited, listening to one stone, heavier than the others, falling against the side of the tumbler as it went on turning slowly like a miniature concrete-mixer.

Mr Varaphan came away from the doorway. 'If you will be so kind . . .' I followed him through the back of the shop, passing

7

some steps in the centre of the house. The piping of the *pi-nai* became louder from above, then faded as we came to the other room. Much of it was taken up with cabinets and safes, but there were some rattan chairs and a table. The walls were timbered and there was the smell of sandalwood. The bleakness of the fluorescent tubes took half the value from a rosewood buddha in the corner but at least you could see where you were. In strange places I hate not being able to see things.

'Your presence in my house does me great honour,' said Mr Varaphan.

'You are most hospitable.' The Westerner suspects the extravagant courtesies of the East and I am always constrained. I added a bit in his own language to please him.

When he left me I noticed three things: there was a telephone in the room; you could make an exit through a second door near the rosewood buddha; and you could still hear quite distinctly the pebbly sound of the gem-tumbler in the shop.

It had been a long trip and I hadn't liked being shot out here without any notice so I tried to relax by looking at the display case on top of one of the safes. It was decent enough stuff: lapis-lazuli, obsidian, rose quartz, a few gem-quality microlites and a very hypnotic moonstone. This place really did belong to a lapidary; it wasn't just a front.

Loman arrived in ten minutes, punctually. He came in by the second door near the buddha, and asked at once:

'When did you get here?'

'A few minutes ago.' We shook hands as perfunctorily as boxers.

'I mean when did you get into Bangkok?'

'This evening at 18.05. Air France Paris–Tokyo –'

'But what were you doing in Paris?'

'Oh my God, is it important?'

'I thought you were still in London when we put out the call for you.' He turned away and turned back, his small feet nervous. 'Everything is important. Very.'

'I hope that includes the fact that I'm here at rendezvous dead on time as per signal, because I'm fed up with bloody aeroplanes –'

'Of course. Of course.' He managed to stand still. There were beads of sweat on his face. 'There was one thing they didn't tell me about this place – there's no air-conditioning.' He was wearing grey alpaca and a spotted bow-tie.

I have a dislike for men with small feet and bow ties and a dislike anyway for Loman. It has been mutual for years but has never affected our work, so that neither considers it important except when we find ourselves shut up together in the confines of a non-air-conditioned lapidary's back room in Bangkok and any other place where it is barely possible to breathe. Loman is like that room in London with the Lowry on the wall: he smells of polish. His shoes and nails and nose shine brightly and even his manners take on a spurious glitter when he has time to rub them up. Just now he was too busy with his nerves.

I was beginning to feel better; seeing him so worried was doing me good. I said: 'Why couldn't they have told me where this door was instead of sending me through the shop?'

'You had to introduce yourself to Varaphan, of course.'

'With that rigmarole?'

'He isn't a contact. We couldn't use established technique.' He was looking around the room, his bright eyes ferreting out the details. 'This is our safe-house for the present. Sometimes we shall meet at the British Embassy but the most important business will take place here. Let us sit down. We will ask for something to be sent in. There is no need for any rush, none at all.'

The rattan creaked under his slight weight and now he was completely relaxed and looking up at me as if it were I whose nerves had been showing.

'Just tell me one thing,' I said. 'Is this a mission or has something come unstuck?'

He tapped the little brass bell on the table.

'It's a mission. And nothing must come unstuck.'

I didn't sit down yet because I was too uneasy with the whole thing. Loman was very high up in the Bureau echelon and he rarely left London to direct an operator in the field. He had never personally directed me before and it wasn't going to be any picnic. I said uncivilly:

'I've just flown seven thousand miles at the drop of a hat and you say there's no rush.'

'Not now that you're *here*.'

It might have been Varaphan's daughter who came in to

answer the bell, a willowy child with a mane of black hair. Loman said to me: 'I haven't very much grasp.'

I told her in English: 'We'd like something to drink, is that possible? Scotch, soda, lime-juice and ice.'

'I will bring, yes.'

'You play the *pi-nai* beautifully.'

She denied it in delight and left us.

'It's the lingua franca,' I told Loman.

'Well you'd better give yourself a crash refresher-course in Thai. You'll be meeting people who don't speak anything else. Also you will want to be able to hear things. How proficient are you?'

'I'm all right outside esoteric terms.'

He got up, feeling restless again. 'What I meant when I said that there was no rush now that you're here is that if you'd been too long delayed we should have had to pull Styles out of Java, and he's very busy there. You know Bangkok as well as he does and you're between missions.'

'Or I was.'

'That's right.'

'It's nearly two years since I was here.' There is a simple tradition in the Bureau that protects any given operation from failure. We can refuse a mission. There has to be a reason and we have to give it and it has to be a good one but in the final analysis we have a get-out if we want it. This is intelligent because it means that nobody is ever sent into the field with misgivings. Any operator taking up a mission has therefore a positive approach and is self-orientated towards success. There is only one thing London Control can do when a man wants to opt out; they have to give him an incentive that will make him opt in again. They tried this on me once in Berlin and it worked: they gave me a man to go after, a man I could hate. Talking now to Loman, I was already putting up the old objection, rationalizing the situation to cover the one main misgiving which was simply that we didn't like each other. The work we had done together in the past was Bureau stuff: intelligence breakdown, communications, liaison, so forth. But now he was going to be my director in the field and that was different because the success of a mission and even your life could sometimes depend on whether you got on well with your director. You had to like him, trust him, respect him and live with him. My opinion of Loman, despite his brilliance and his record, was that he was a well-polished little pimp. It didn't help that he looked on me as a rough-haired sheepdog with more guts than gumption, a chip on each shoulder and one on the wick.

'After two years,' I told him, 'I don't remember much about this place.'

'You will now that you're back.'

His point. The memory relies strongly on environment. Recollective recall. If examinations were taken in the familiar surroundings of the lecture-rooms *where the stuff was learned* there would be fewer failures.

'I don't know this place for a start. Who's Varaphan?'

'The Embassy gave us his name.'

'Don't tell me you trust the Embassy.'

'We've checked on him, of course. He was educated on the Burma Road, liaising with our escape-parties. Since then he's been useful, very useful, to several of our operations. He travels a lot, with gems. That takes him to London a great deal.'

'He's not an agent?'

'Not strictly.'

'He took a good look at the street to see if I'd been followed before bringing me in here.'

'He's not a fool.'

We had to stop talking because the girl was coming in with the drinks. As soon as she had gone we set on the lime-juice.

'At least he could rig up a fan in here,' I said.

'We will see what can be done.'

Some of the mutual antagonism went out of us now that our thirst was slaked.

'Is this Local Control Bangkok?'

He considered. 'We don't quite know where Control is yet. It's officially at the Embassy, though of course they don't know that. They think we're Security. This is our safe-house for the moment but if things get too hot we shall have to move on.'

My ears were still buzzing a bit from the altitude and I had come straight here from Don Muang Airport with no time to change into fresh things, so I said:

'Let's put it on the line, shall we?'

He was nervous again at once and I knew he'd been holding me off because he sensed I would try to refuse the mission, and that would mean pulling Styles out of Java.

He poured some more lime to give himself a last chance of planning his run-in.

'This is a special job,' he began. 'Very.'

I fingered a chunk of ice out of my glass and sucked it while he turned away and looked at the rosewood buddha and turned back and at last managed to stand still plumb in front of me. 'You may know there is an official visit planned for the end of this month. Three days in Bangkok as part of a larger South-East Asian itinerary.'

'No,' I said.

'You don't read the newspapers.'

'Not often.'

'Then let me put you in the picture. Politically – one can even say militarily in view of local wars – Thailand is becoming drawn into the vortex of affairs involving China, India, Malaysia and of course Laos and Cambodia. Global interest is now centred on this capital, which has been a focal point in South-East Asia for half a century in any case. Thailand is a stable kingdom with close ties with the US and to a lesser extent with Britain. We have NATO here in this city and we have the SEATO headquarters here as well. Bangkok is a key city in the South-East Asian complex, and geographically it finds itself in the middle of the China–India situation.'

Loman is one of those people who make whatever they are saying sound dull. Perhaps I was showing boredom: he began talking faster so that he could reach the point.

'Relations between Britain and Thailand have always been good, partly because each is a democratic monarchy and partly because many people close to the Thai throne – princes, ministers, financiers and men of affairs – spent much of their youth in English public schools and universities. At this time, when the whole of the South-East Asian picture is confused and threatening, Her Majesty's Government consider it highly desirable that a goodwill mission is undertaken by someone who is neither a statesman nor a diplomat but who commands international respect and admiration, particularly in Thailand.'

He waited for me to digest this. Some of his nervousness had gone; it had been soothed away by the reassuring sound of his own voice.

'Thus in three weeks' time a representative of the Queen is to visit Bangkok on a goodwill tour.'

Most of the ice in the bowl had melted but I found a bit and slaked my thirst with it.

'Since the Person – by the way, that is how we already refer to him for security reasons, so please adopt the habit – since the Person is neither a statesman nor a diplomat a tour of this kind entails no political functions. There will be, instead, a day's yachting on the Gulf, a polo match at the Lumpini Grounds – I am told that Prince Udom is to play – and a drive through the city in an open car. The Person will also visit those centres of traditional interest to him: youth clubs, welfare organizations, hospitals and of course sports grounds. He will be, one might say, our representative of the humanities.'

With careful precision he said:

'During the visit we want you to arrange for his assassination.'

Chapter Two

PANGSAPA

The two fish circled, their heads turned towards the centre to watch each other.

The smaller was the more beautiful, its colours less diffuse, but both were caparisoned in the flowing splendour of their fins. They moved like rainbows through the pearly water. Faintly reflected in the glass was the face of Pangsapa, an enormous moon.

The strange sweet smell of opium was in the air.

The fish sped suddenly together, dart-quick and murderous, with the fins drawn close to the body as they met – a torn fin could unbalance them and bring almost immediate death.

The eyes of Pangsapa were unblinking in the great moon on the glass.

The fish circled near the sides of the tank with their coloured raiment flowing, like medieval war-horses on the battlefield. The next charge was mutual and explosive – they closed, met, held and spun in a whirlpool, with their razor-teeth working for a kill. Three times they attacked and withdrew, and now the water was tinged with carmine and from the spine of the smaller and more beautiful fish curled a crimson plume. As the water clouded with their blood, the face of Pangsapa was reflected more brightly. Once his eyes flicked towards me and flicked back: he wanted to feel that I shared his terrible delight.

A red plume streaked towards the centre; a rose-dark blossom spread and slowly spun, ushering upwards the vanquished. It floated on the surface, silver beneath the light. It was the smaller and the more beautiful.

Pangsapa turned away.

'That was Valiant Warlord,' he lisped. 'He had won seven fights, one of them against Golden Prince of Maipuri, the champion of a friend of mine. Such is the outcome.'

Knowing that his invitation for me to watch the fight was a courtesy rarely offered a stranger, I said:

'It was well fought. I was fascinated.'

He gestured for me to sit again on the cushions near him. 'Will you smoke?' Two or three opium-pipes were on the gold-lacquered stool.

'I am not accustomed, Pangsapa, but please take your pleasure.'

'My pleasure is already assured, since you honour me as a guest.' He sat with his legs crossed under him in the Lotus pose, his black silk robe enfolding him. The cushions made the only colour in the room except for the rose-red water tank. Three black orchids were grouped in a Niello bowl; a Phuan-Sadao tapestry in ash-grey tones was spread on the wall; the rest was teakwood and ebony.

He called a name suddenly and a servant came.

'Arrange for the burial of the fish. I will attend the ceremony.'

When the man had gone Pangsapa said in English: 'And while we're on the subject of guests I really can't let you go on speaking Thai in my house, though of course you do it splendidly.'

'I wanted to brush up my subjunctives.'

Loman had told me to take a crash refresher-course and I had been compromising, talking to everyone in the Bangkok dialect even when they just as resolutely stuck to Boston English.

'Your subjunctives are first class. Now you must let me have a go with mine.' There was something wistful about his smile and he looked younger still, a fat boy in the part of Buddha in a school play, a boy with a lisp. 'Tell me first how I can help you.'

I took a few seconds to think. Loman had told me that he could be useful to us, 'very'. All I knew about Pangsapa was that he was in 'Import-Export', the classic cover-name for illegal traffick-ing. He was a link between a dozen warehouse operators along the Chao Phraya River. Since Bangkok is the principal world source of illegal opium there are many people in Import-Export; the Chao Phraya, like most rivers, flows to the sea.

Loman had said: 'We haven't made contact with Pangsapa before but he is said to be a good source of information. He knows a lot of people outside the law who might turn up in your search-area and he might feel ready to hand some of them to us on a plate, either because they're his competitors or because we put a decent price on them. So far nobody's found out what he will *not* do for money.'

We had talked for another hour at the safe-house in Soi Suek 3, Loman and I. His bit about my making arrangements for the assassination had caught my interest at last, but I didn't say anything.

'I'm sure you get the point,' Loman said.

'I'm to make the arrangements and then give you the set-up so that you can take counter-measures against any similar plan.'

'That's right.'

'It's bloody silly. You can plan it a dozen ways.'

'We think your way would be the most efficient. We think we are up against somebody very clever. Don't misunderstand me: I am not buttering you up so that you'll co-operate.' His smile was smooth. 'You don't want this mission, or *any* mission with me as your intelligence director in the field. We don't like each other, do we? But I was asked in London to choose a man who could plan this kind of job – an assassination – so efficiently that it couldn't fail. I think you'll agree that there's more at stake than a few hard words between us if we do this job together. So I chose you.'

I said: 'You'll just have to go on talking. Get me out of the dark. I suppose there's been a threat, has there?'

'Of course.'

'Then why don't they just call it off?'

'The visit? For the same reason that they didn't call off the Queen's visit to Canada. Your Anglo-Saxon doesn't panic easily. Also this visit is part, as I told you, of a larger itinerary in South-East Asia. They can't leave out Bangkok because it's the most important stop. And they can't cancel the whole thing because of one threat in one place. Even if the Government decided to back out I doubt if the Person would let them – he's not quite the type. So we're all in it.' He drank off the rest of the lime in his glass and looked at me again and asked silkily: 'Or aren't you included?'

'Oh for God's sake stop mucking about and give me the guts of the thing so I can make up my mind. I don't know a bloody tenth of what's going on, do I?'

But I knew more now than he'd told me. I knew why he'd arrived with his nerves in the upper register: this kind of mission wasn't in his line. He is a specialist in short-range penetration operations with a disciplined cell and planned access and good communications – not such a pushover as it sounds, if the opposition is the best. He is brilliant at it: five adverse agents neutralized in the European area and two on home ground sent down for a fourteen-year stretch (the Kingston net), all in the past eighteen months.

Why had Control sent him out here on a lark like this?

He was still smiling gently. He knew I was angry because I was interested and therefore afraid of being coerced into this mission. Someone had said in that room with the Lowry: 'He won't fall easily for this one unless we can sting him up. Send someone out there he doesn't like, someone who'll get his goat.'

Loman was perfect casting.

'Let me give you the other nine-tenths,' he said equably. 'This is of course a job for Security and a few people have been flown out here quietly to help take care of the threat and its implications. The Thai Home Office is being very co-operative and – '

'Wait a minute. What sort of threat was it?'

'It was sent by ordinary letter to London, written in English. It said simply that if the Person came to this city he wouldn't leave it alive. Of course the Yard has taken the letter apart in Forensic and sent a couple of people out here to confer with the Thai CID. They are working on it now.'

'All right.'

'As I say, the Home Office is being very helpful and all the routine enquiries and searches are under way. The UK is well represented, unofficially.'

'Who roped in the Bureau, then?'

'The Bureau was not *roped in*,' he said stuffily. 'Certain information came in and it was decided that action was indicated. No fewer than eight directives were planned and examined before the decision was formalized. This is the ninth, and it has now become a definite mission. Because the Bureau thinks – I do hope you feel they are right – that we should do something to ensure that nothing happens on the day. They consider the Person to be – how shall I say? – rather valuable.'

I mentally blasted him and his ninth directive to hell, got a clean glass and began on the whisky. This approach of Loman's was deliberate: I was meant to feel frightfully un-British if I didn't immediately choke with rage at the thought of anything happening to our Valuable Person. The Bureau could have spared a minute in sober thought: I always like a clear field to work in and I work best alone, and if they were sending me into a mission

17

where the UK was already 'well represented', they would risk my fouling up the whole operation by getting in the way.

The only thing to do was to let him go on giving it to me until I had the complete picture and then say yes or no.

'Of course,' he said smoothly, 'you will be working alone. Quite alone.'

They'd sent the right man, give them that. He knew me to the bone.

'This isn't a joint operation, you see. How could it be? The Bureau doesn't exist. It never has. No, the idea is very simple. Unless they're unlucky, the security branches will make quite certain that nothing happens on the visit. They are planning every conceivable precaution. But there may be a thousand-to-one chance that the adverse party will organize a plan that will come off. A plan so efficient that there is *no* counter-measure possible. A plan – as I suggested to Control – that only *you* could devise.'

He began walking about, talking as if there would be no interruption. Perhaps he was trying to convince himself of the mechanics of this thing before he could successfully sell it to me.

'This isn't blandishment, you see. Your work in Egypt, Cuba and Berlin has proved that if you're left on your own when things are sufficiently hot you are capable of pulling off a certain *kind* of operation at which a dozen better men or a hundred better men would fail, simply because it's an operation requiring one man working alone and requiring the *kind* of man who works best alone. That is why you were chosen.' He stopped in front of the display case and stared at the moonstone until his feet couldn't keep still any more. He came back to stand in front of me. 'There is nothing else I can tell you until the information starts coming in from the Foreign Office. You'll be in on every conference at the Embassy here and we shall – '

'This isn't in your field, Loman.' I was suddenly fed up with him. 'And it's not in mine. It's no go.'

'You need time to think.'

'I've thought. This is a police job. I'm a penetration agent – '

'If you want to play with terms – '

'It's no go. Tell them they've made a mistake – '

'I don't think they have. I chose you myself – '

'Then it's your own mistake – '

18

'I don't think it is – '

'Tell them to pull Styles out of Java – '

'No, it's you I want for this one, Quiller. You.'

He wasn't smiling any more and all the polish had gone to his eyes. They were very bright.

'Let's get it over with,' he said. 'It would take too long for *you* to tell me what you think of me and it wouldn't affect the issue because I'm mud-proof. In *my* unfortunate experience you've proved yourself an agent who is obstinate, undisciplined, illogical and dangerously prone to obsessive vanities and wild cat tactics, very difficult to handle in the field and an embarrassment in London whenever you choose to report there in person. If you accept this mission – and you will accept it – I shall be your director and will be responsible for everything you do, so there's nothing in this for me but a filthy time of it the whole way through and I settle for that here and now. That is my position. This is yours: you now have information that a man revered in his own country and respected abroad is going to have the guts to expose himself to a threat of death because he won't refuse his duty. You also know that *if* the very elaborate machinery for his protection breaks down and *if* this valuable life is lost because of your own petty feelings against me as your director in the field, it's going to be your fault – your fault alone. And you won't be able to live with it.'

He gazed at me with his eyes shining and I knew I had never hated him more than I did then. In a minute he half-turned, fiddling about on the table, saying:

'I see you've hogged the last of the ice. That's typical.' He banged the bell. 'So you can't refuse this mission. I knew that when I left London. You can't refuse. When that man arrives in Bangkok you'll be here with him right in the thick of it. So you'd better lay into me and then we'll have another drink and then I'll brief you. We haven't long.'

Chapter Three

KUO

The English word 'assassin' is borrowed from the French but stems originally from the Arabic *hashshashin*, meaning 'hashish-eaters'.

There were two good reasons why Loman had given me Pangsapa as a possible informant. Modern man will take great risks for money and greater risks for sex; but when he has need of drugs he will hazard himself most fearfully of all. Driven beyond all caution he will expose, sell and surrender himself to the despotic sovereignty of men like Pangsapa.

Pangsapa was a narcotics contrabandist and would therefore know people who were prepared to kill for a fix of snow, or who were prepared to expose the most sacrosanct confidences of friends and inform on them.

We wanted information and we wanted information about assassins; so Loman had sent me here.

He knew in addition that the only good contact I had ever had in this city was dead, because that evening on Rama IV Road in the poor light they had mistaken him for me.

Pangsapa wanted to talk and I let him.

'I remember when your Princess Alexandra made a visit here a few years ago. It went off marvellously. Everyone loved her on sight and we coined a new title for her – the Gentle Ambassadress. She's having the same success with her current excursions; and last year she went over wonderfully in Tokyo. It's so intelligent of the British to send *interesting* people abroad as a change from those dreary diplomats with rumpled waistcoats and Derby winners' teeth.'

I hadn't told him why I had come. Loman must have given him a hint. I had only one question for him: where were the professionals? But he wanted to go on talking.

'You may think it odd that I hold such an affection for members of the British royalty. After all I was born in poverty. I remember very clearly the time when I was beaten by a merchant for thieving – my choice was to steal or starve in those days. It happened when I was ostensibly watching a state procession on the river, with the Royal Barge and all the trimmings. Have you ever seen that barge, the *Sri Supanahongs*? It's quite enormous and covered entirely with pure gold leaf. The bag of rice I was filching at the time on one of the market canals was half-soaked in filthy water but it kept me alive for six days.' He smiled wistfully. 'It wasn't likely to endear me to the monarchy, my own or any other. But events happen so quickly. Not long afterwards my father – or the man I believe to be my father – began toying with a certain hazardous operation in cahoots with a ship's captain, and the wind turned out to be fair. Five years later I was at Oxford, of all places.'

He sat with remarkable stillness and his smile was seraphic. 'My degree is in Economics. But I cherish far more the spiritual experience the life of your country vouchsafed me. It was in those years that I learned to bear a certain love for complete strangers – I'm talking again of the monarchy.'

He leaned towards me an inch and his lisp became pronounced 'I would be sorry if anything happened in a few weeks' time on the 29th.'

'You might be able to prevent it.'

'I would welcome the chance.'

'All I want to know is where the professionals are. If any of them are *here*. In Bangkok.'

'The professionals?'

I got up from the cushions to walk about. Maybe he hadn't been briefed fully enough. 'Did Loman come to see you?'

'I don't know that name.'

'Who told you I was coming?'

'No one.'

I stopped and stood looking down at him.

'You didn't expect me.'

'Not before you telephoned.' He sat like a small dark effigy, only the light in his yellow eyes showing that he was alive.

I said: 'All right, Pangsapa. What was all that about your undying love for the monarchy?'

Patiently he said: 'You forget that the whole city is preparing for this important visit on the 29th. The police and security branches are very active, and it is obvious that trouble is expected

21

– specific trouble. What else could you have come about? You seek information.'

I said: 'You've never seen me before.'

'You have been in Bangkok before.'

I accepted that. He'd been given to me as a source of information and no source of information was much good if it had never heard about my job here two years ago. I pressed him, though:

'Have you ever been in contact with us before?'

'I know a man called Parkis.'

'All right.' Parkis was in London Control. 'Let's talk about the professionals. I want to know their travel-patterns.'

He looked perplexed. 'I'm not quite sure what you mean by the "professionals" – '

'I mean Vincent – Sorbi – Kuo – '

'Quicky the Greek – Hideo – the Mafia boy, what's his name?'

'Zotta.'

'That's it – Zotta.'

I relaxed again. He hadn't denied knowing Zotta. The Mafia channelled most of their stuff from Bangkok through Naples to Recife now that the Buenos Aires route was blocked following the death of Primero, and it was Zotta who did the bump. Pangsapa would know about that. It was his business.

Zotta is in Recife,' he said. 'You can forget him. 'He stood up suddenly and without effort, without even taking his hands from the folds of his robe.

'Vincent?'

'He's in prison in Athens. They're getting him out, of course, but that will take longer than three weeks because his people are disorganized.'

'Sorbi?'

His hands appeared, pale against the black robe. 'Who ever knows where Sorbi is?'

'Kuo? Hideo? The Greek?'

'When I have had a little time,' he said, 'I will get in touch with you. I know that the information would be valuable to you.'

'It depends.' London is precise on this. When you go shopping you have to do a bargain when you can.

'We can arrange it later,' he shrugged. 'Where can I find you?'

'Pakchong Hotel.'

As we went towards the door I noticed the water in the tank was clear again, changed by the filter-flow system. The fish swam alone, a six-inch compact rainbow-coloured killer. A professional.

In two days I was ready to tell Loman the mission was refused. It was a security job and that wasn't in my field. The place was slopping over with security people anyway and any one of them could handle this thing better than I could: they knew the formula and they were trained to work with it.

I had gone to see Pangsapa because I might need him one day if a real mission ever brought me back to Bangkok. There'd been no point in *not* sounding him on the travel-patterns of the professionals: I always like to know where people are. But if his sources were as good as Loman believed, he would have contacted me by now even if only to report on their whereabouts. He would know that London would cough up a little even for negative information. But he obviously couldn't get any.

It was no go. The thing had no shape. I was drifting about the city without even a decent cover or a cover-story and every time I checked for tags there weren't any because no one wanted to know where I went or what I was doing.

I knew why Loman had called me in. It was typical of him. He hadn't given any real answer when I'd asked him who roped the Bureau in. He'd done it himself: sold this abortive scheme to Parkis and the others and chosen me for the field. He must have talked well. His whole project was based on the spurious premise of a threat. Anyone planning an assassination would never put out a threat before the attempt; all it would do would be to alert the security forces, and that was precisely what it had done. Security was geared to combat any action by a psychopath, reasonably enough: there were always psychopaths in the crowd whenever a VIP did the rounds. The Pope's visit to New York in 1965 put eighteen thousand city police on special duty, with bomb-squads combing the route and riflemen manning the roof-tops, simply because of a few letters from anonymous religious eccentrics.

This was routine work. The Bureau never took that kind of thing on: it was set up to promote specific operations. Why the hell had they listened to Loman?

23

I tried contacting him through Soi Suek 3 but he hadn't shown up since the day I flew in so I went to the Embassy and asked for Room 6. He had said it was all right for me to do that.

The young man looked nervous.

'Room 6?'

'Yes.'

'That will be Miss Maine, won't it?'

'Will it?'

'If you'll just take a seat.'

I watched him making tentative hops towards the next office. He hadn't even asked for my name.

If Loman was in Room 6 I would tell him I knew why he'd roped in the Bureau and why he'd roped in me, then watch his face.

The Harrow type came back and took me along the passage into another room. The door said 'Cultural Attaché'. I was alone five minutes and a girl came in, a woman – I never know their age.

'Can I help you?'

'Do you know where I find Room 6?'

She looked at me a long time. I didn't mind. The staffs of embassies always need a few days to put one thought after another. It's almost relaxing.

'There's nobody there at the moment. Perhaps I can help you.'

'Are you the Cultural Attaché?'

'His secretary.'

'Well that schoolboy hasn't got his sums right. I want Room 6. If that doesn't mean anything I want to see a man named Loman.'

'Mr Loman isn't here.'

'Oh for the Lord's *sake*. Well if you ever see him just tell him I've tried contacting him all afternoon and now I'm taking the night-plane on the London run.'

Undisciplined behaviour. Tell it to the Lowry.

'Just a moment, please.'

She walked well and had a calm clear voice. I found it mollifying. Maybe that was what she was there for, to stop people blowing up about the malorganization.

A man came in next and she wasn't with him. He shut the door and offered his hand. 'Have a chair?'

'All right,' I said, 'they're all yours.' I dropped my papers on to the desk. With the flap on about the 29th they were probably security-checking the Ambassador himself every time he came back from the lavatory.

Now I knew why no one had asked for my name. Names don't mean a thing.

He gave the papers a quick run through. 'You're based where . . . exactly?' He peered at page 2 as if he couldn't read the writing. I said:

'Whitehall 9. Liaison Group. Lovett sees to me.'

'Ah, yes Lovett. How is he these days?' He pushed a cigarette-box across. 'Like to smoke?'

'He's very well.' To save time I went through the lot. 'He was in Rome last week on the Carosio thing and Bill Spencer took over in London. Your boys were Simms and Westlake. They – '

'That's all right, yes. But I thought you were there too.'

'It says Paris on my passport, doesn't it?'

He pulled back the cigarette-box and lit one. 'Are you going to be in Bangkok long?'

'No.'

'No?'

'I'm flying out tonight unless Loman turns up.'

'He won't be here until tomorrow.'

'Then give him my love.' I stood up and held out my hand for the papers. He said with a wrinkled smile:

'I'm surprised you're not staying.'

'You don't need me here. You'll do all right.'

'If you don't mind I'll ask Miss Maine to show you out.'

'I know my way.'

It was stinking hot in the street and I took a trishaw back to the Pakchong, trying not to think about Loman. When you're meant to be directing someone in the field you don't slide off and subject him to security checks.

At the hotel the desk called me twenty minutes later and said my visitor would not give a name, so I went down. I don't like nameless people in my room.

The lobby of the Pakchong has one of those beautiful trellis arches at the entrance to the fountain court and she was standing framed by it, her lean body sideways on, her throat shadowed by the angle of her head as she looked across to the staircase, her eyes regarding me coolly, as they had before. A Shantung suit, tan shoes, no jewellery.

Only her head moved as I crossed the mosaic. The place was very quiet and she pitched her voice low.

'May I use your name?'

'Nobody knows it,' I said.

'Your cover-name.'

'Who cares?'

'I came to apologize, Mr Quiller. I should have recognized you at the Embassy.'

'I'm not often recognized by the secretaries of cultural attachés. Yehudi Menuhin's more their type.'

'I wasn't far from Rama IV two years ago.'

Now that I was close to her I could see that something had happened to her face on the left side. It didn't quite balance. The skin was perfect but someone – someone very good – had done a job on it.

'What are you?' I asked her. 'Mil. 6?'

She didn't answer, didn't seem interested. I said:

'Not Security.'

'No.' She changed the slim tan bag into the other hand. 'I just came to apologize. You can't be used to the indignity of security checks.'

I didn't quite laugh. 'You'd be surprised at the indignities I'm used to.' Along with Dewhurst and Comyngs my cover name on file had the 9-suffix: Reliable Under Torture. 'Will you have a drink?'

'I can't stay. They say you're leaving tonight.'

'Yes.'

'Have a good trip.'

I watched her cross the mosaic. Not many women can walk like that when they know a man's watching them. Not many women can walk like that anyway.

I went up and finished packing. To apologize? She couldn't have thought that one up for herself; she was too intelligent. Why had they wanted to know that I was physically and in all truth at the Pakchong Hotel? They could have checked on me in a dozen better ways.

Blast their eyes, I was on Flight 204.

The only other thing that happened that day was a phone-call from Pangsapa, asking me to go along to his house.

It was dark but most of the shops were still open and some of them were already re-dressing the windows with coloured bunting and gold-framed photographs of the Person.

I had the trishaw drop me some distance from the house in Klong Chula Road and walked along the river in the evening heat. Pangsapa received me straight away and said:

'The information I have for you is worth something in the region of fifty thousand *baht*.'

It was too late but I didn't say so. It would be amusing to milk Loman's expense account and let them fry him when he got back to London.

'Fifty thousand,' I said. 'All right.'

'You can guarantee that sum?'

'Verbally, yes.'

'Your word is quite sufficient.'

I knew now that I shouldn't have come. It was a lot of money and it would be a lot of information and I didn't want it, didn't want to be involved.

Pangsapa said softly: 'Three days ago one of the "professionals" crossed over the Mekong River from Laos into Thailand and tonight he arrived in Bangkok.'

'Which one?'

'Kuo the Mongolian.'

So there was nothing I could do about it now.

Chapter Four

THE SPECIALISTS

They are specialists and each has his own method.

Sorbi is a strangler but never uses his hands: it is nearly always a nylon stocking, infrequently a cord. He is a lecher and runs with the night-club set in European capital cities, finding most of his work there. He calls himself a 'private' operator: half his kills are women and he is offered his work by rich men or men of high position who cannot afford exposure. Sorbi was behind the 'Blue Room Mystery' of the June 1964 Paris headlines (Mme Latrelle-Voisin) and the 'Autostrada Angel Case' in Milan, 1965, which led to the resignation of three members of the Italian Government. (Sorbi's client was not, of course, implicated.) This operation brought Sorbi into touch with politicals and he is now said to hold himself available for political work, the fees being very high.

Quicky the Greek uses the knife and has made only two killings, but both were important and both political and so well arranged that in one case (the leader of the 'Interim' Bolivian Cabinet) the record still shows a verdict of suicide. The Greek never asks for money but for deeds of title, and he is said to own fifteen thousand acres of land in the key development areas of the Argentine and Venezuela. He may not live long to enjoy his possessions, as Pangsapa himself told me that Quicky is hooked on snow.

Vincent works wild and nobody trusts him, though he is so persistent that once a name is given to him the man of that name can be considered as dead. Vincent will use anything – a gun or a knife, poison, a bomb or his bare hands. Also he is cheap, and they say he would work even for nothing. (He was behind the *coup d'état* in Egypt when Lieutenant-Colonel Ibrahim was found locked in his Cadillac at the bottom of the Nile – a dredger had struck the obstacle.)

The Japanese, Hideo, is a technician and one hundred per cent efficient. He always uses a cyanide spray, possibly impressed by the clinical success of the KGB agent Bogdan Stashinski who in

1961 acknowledged the killing of Rebet and Bandera (leaders of the Ukrainian émigrés) in Munich, 1957. Hideo has three major political assassinations on record, including that of the Turkish Ambassador to the United Kingdom (the 'Gold Pencil Murder' – the finding of the victim's gold pencil on the pavement in Curzon Street led to the discovery of his body in an abandoned taxi in Wallace Mews). Hideo the technician has the most elaborate model railway in Japan.

Zotta is the son of one of the Mafia's original 'Murder Inc.' group and his speciality is the miniature bomb. He claims that his weapon is 'personalized' and that accurate placing will ensure a quick clean kill with no danger to anybody else in the vicinity of the victim. This is probably true: When Sherman Wills, president of the Charter and Equity Bank, opened his pen in the boardroom at the start of a meeting (New York, 1963) nobody else was hurt. A year later the half-brother of King Riyadh Ali switched on his electric shaver in the royal yacht standing off Damascus and the stateroom windows remained unbroken. Zotta is a technician like Hideo but far less stable. When he dies there will be a woman there who will not grieve.

They are all specialists and each has his own method.

Kuo uses the gun.

Pangsapa was very good. He sent someone with me – a small nervous Hindu half-scared of himself or of someone, perhaps of Pangsapa – to find Kuo the Mongolian and look at him.

He was watching the professional Karate training-bouts in the gymnasium of the Royal Thai Athletic Association, not far from the Lumpini polo grounds. A fight was in progress and we chose seats beside the main entrance. The place was air-conditioned but smelled of embrocation, resin and sweat. My guide sat for a few minutes idly watching the spectators and suddenly looked down, murmuring: 'He is in the second row up, half-way along on the right side. He is the one in smoked glasses.'

By his tone I knew that it was Kuo he was scared of.

I slowly raised my eyes.

'You can go now,' I said. 'If you are certain.'

'Yes. I knew him well once.'

I looked down again at the fighters until the Hindu had gone, in case his movement were noticed. Then I looked across again at Kuo. Even if my guide had not pointed him out I would have known him for what he was: a man of authority, a man of affairs. He was in European clothes, a white Tergal suit impeccably cut and worn with indifference, a dark-blue tie with a gold motif, small gold cuff-links. His authority was in the way he sat, in the angle of his body and the poise of his head. Nothing of this was deliberate; he was engrossed in the fight. On each side of him sat a bodyguard, dressed also in Western clothes. Their deference was as explicit as his authority.

I wished I could see his eyes. I would have to recognize him later, recognize him immediately even at a distance, even in bad light. The eyes are so important – the eyes and the walk. I would have to stay until he left, so that I could see him walk.

The feet of the Karate fighters stamped. You could hear their breath. They were the Thai champions and would fight here during the Visit. Their shadows fought on the resined boards under their feet, sharply thrown by the grouped lamps.

Sometimes Kuo was tense and I remembered Pangsapa watching the fish; sometimes he tilted his compact head and laughed with one of the bodyguards. He was enjoying himself.

I watched him for an hour, every gesture, every movement of his head. When some people came into my row I got up and sidled between the seats with my back to the arena and made my way round the end of the gymnasium, finding a seat above and to one side of Kuo so that I could impress his back view on my memory: tomorrow I would begin to follow him, to live with him and learn him until I knew him as if he were my brother.

When he left the gymnasium I watched him walk across the clear space at the end where there were no seats. It was a good walk; his arms swung easily, the hands relaxed; he placed his feet with deliberation, his head half-turned attentively, as one of his men spoke to him. He could have been a president leaving the conference-hall. He reached the doors and I let him go. If he did not come here again tomorrow Pangsapa could find him. Then I would take over.

First thing in the morning I telephoned Varaphan and told him I wanted the bloodstone ready as soon as possible. Loman rang me within the hour and I went down to Soi Suek 3. He looked wary.

'They said you were flying out.'

'I'm not,' I said.

'What changed your mind?'

'Do you know who arrived in Bangkok yesterday?'

'Pangsapa told me.'

'What made you see Pangsapa? I thought you meant to keep clear.'

'I meant to, yes. Then I heard you were restive so I wanted to know if he'd turned anything up.'

'I was getting bloody tired of trying to contact you and I didn't like being vetted at the Embassy. Who's that woman they've got there?'

He said curiously, 'There are quite a few women – '

'She's in the Cultural Attaché's office. Is she Mil. 6 or Security or what?'

'You mean Vinia Maine, I think.'

'She in our group?'

'Oh no.'

'Well tell her to keep out of my way. She had me checked and then followed me. I don't like her. Listen,' I said, 'I'm accepting the mission but on my own terms. This job isn't in your field but you roped in the Bureau the minute you caught wind of this thing because there's the chance of a tin medal, isn't there?' I was watching his face. 'If anything comes unstuck on the Visit and it's left to me to stop Kuo there'll be credit owed in high places and you know what I think of medals – but *someone's* going to cop one and you're ready at the head of the queue, the Bureau's director in the field who pulled the whole thing off.'

His eyes were very bright and he kept perfectly still, looking back at me, shining with hate.

I said: 'That's all right. All I want you to get quite clear is that I'm not working for *you*. I'm working for *him*. Because I don't like to think of a decent man with a wife and kids getting shot in the guts and I don't care if he's the postman or the King of Hong Kong. Now I'll tell you my terms.'

He moved away and put both hands on the glass top of the display-case, leaning on it and looking in at the gems. But he was listening.

'You said there'll be conferences at the Embassy. Count me out. I'm working alone. But I'll need up-to-the-minute information from you that I won't have time to get for myself – arrival schedules for the 29th, programme and final itinerary for the tour of the city, stopping-off points, so forth. If things get hot I want to be put into contact with you at a minute's notice whether it's here or a new safe-house. Unless there's any change of plan I want to be left alone.'

He stood for a while leaning on the case and then turned to me and asked: 'Is that all?'

'Yes.'

'What have you in mind?' His tone was even. I was a louse and he was interested in lice and wanted to know how they worked.

'Kuo. That's all I've got in mind. You know his reputation: he's top in his class as a long-range rifleman and he's never been known to miss.'

He nodded. 'Pangsapa tells me he has come to Bangkok simply to watch the Karate fights – they'll be putting on a very special show, of course, and he's a keen *aficionado*. It may be true. We shall just assume he's here to attempt an assassination and work on that.'

'You've briefed me to make the arrangements and give you the set-up and that's what I'm going to do. First I've got to learn the man and try getting his local travel-patterns. If I'm in luck I might even get a lead on *his* arrangements – they'll be more efficient than mine, he's done it before.'

'I suppose,' he said carefully, 'you have been giving some thought to the threat – the actual threat received in London.'

'It wasn't from Kuo. It wasn't from anyone who means to have a go. I'm not interested.'

'Of course it was valuable to us. We wouldn't have been alerted otherwise. We wouldn't be here now, you and I.'

With no rancour I said: 'What a bloody shame.'

He smiled quickly. He'd swallowed the hate. It was still there all right and one fine day he would catch me wide open and slam me down or try to.

'You'll need to know the security picture,' he said. 'It's not easy for me to get information in that area. We don't exist and we've no official access or liaison. Also they're cagey by nature. But I know this much: they're keeping three suspects in view. One is of course Kuo himself, but they don't rate him very highly. Kuo is respected and the moment he crosses a frontier they double the security guard round the head of state as a matter of routine. On the other hand he travels a great deal even when he's – shall we say – off duty. Providing he remains in view and doesn't go to ground, they'll be content to keep a routine watch on him. If he goes to ground they'll try to find him but they'll use routine methods and it might be too late. But you will have been concentrating solely on him and with any luck you'll know where he's gone.' He gave me one of his bright stares. 'Don't ever lose him, will you?'

'And I won't eat too many sweets.' They were all like that, the London mob. Talked to you like a bloody governess.

'Remember,' he said in precisely the same tone, 'that the Thai Home Office and Security departments have been told of the threat received in London and are giving our people unlimited facilities. King Aduldej has been kept informed and has made it very clear that he expects every conceivable effort to be made for the protection of his guest. Quite apart from anything else he is jealous of his capital city's reputation as a place where one can walk in the streets unharmed.'

When Loman wasn't talking like a governess he was talking like an official spokesman for the Junior Conservative Society. I went on listening.

'The city police are already mounting a dragnet operation to round up all known or suspected agitators and subversives. The first wave of arrests will take place in two days' time. Routine checks are already going on at Don Muang Airport, the Royal Palace and the major stopping-off points along the route the motorcade will take. All mail and messages addressed to the Person to await his arrival are being given the infra-red and there is a permanent police guard in the Palace kitchens and garage. The guest suite now being prepared is – '

'Look,' I said wearily, 'it's up to them what they do. There's a dozen ways – prussic acid in the caviar, the parcel-bomb, the snake-in-the-mattress trick. But you've told me yourself that we've got to assume that Kuo has been sent in to do this job, so let me concentrate on him. As far as I'm concerned it's going to be the classic method, the one that's most difficult to stop – the long-shot. A public execution.'

Chapter Five

GROUND

A simple rule of mnemonics is that if a face is to be remembered it must be forgotten in its absence. Attempted recall in the absence of the image is dangerously prone to distort it.

A man of sour disposition and small stature may have a short grey beard and vivid skin-coloration; these two features are easily accepted on sight by the memory. But later, in the absence of the image, the memory will concentrate on the only data in its possession and exaggerate: the beard will become longer and whiter, the face rosier. Small additions to the image then build up, since the need to remember flogs the mechanism that must do it; the eyes are now remembered as being light blue, the figure as large and lumbering – now the man is certain to be remembered the next time he is seen.

In fact he is not even recognized. In place of the almost wholly fictional image of Santa Claus's twin brother is the real thing: a small, irascible man with brown eyes and a tobacco-stained grey beard.

Most instances of poor memory are examples of retroactive interference producing qualitative changes: the memory, goaded into conscious service, begins making things up. If left alone, the initial neural traces will remain absolutely clear, and will recognize the image immediately the next time it is seen – because no change has taken place.

Kuo the Mongolian was a difficult image partly because he was Mongolian and partly because his features were not typically Mongoloid. He could have passed for a Manchurian, a Sikhote Alinese, a Kunlunese or even a Cantonese. So I made no attempt to remember him after establishing the initial image in the gymnasium. There was thus no remoulding of the recall process.

Recognition was immediate the next day when he came out of the gymnasium just before noon. I knew there were training-fights each morning and evening this week and I was waiting for him.

The machine I had chosen from Compact Hire was tailor-made for the work in hand: a 1500 Toyota Corona with a 90 m.p.h. peak and a 19·7 quarter-mile standing-start performance. Being small, it could cope with even a New Road rush-hour tangle; being fast it could keep most other cars in sight along the exurban fringe highways even if they were trying to slip the tag.

The windscreen was raked only a few degrees and the facia-top reflection across the lens of my field-glasses was not serious. I had Kuo in them at ×8 magnification as he came down the steps.

We started from there.

For six days he made no attempt, absolutely no attempt, to hide his movements. This worried me. He was too accommodating. I didn't like his display of confidence. I knew – and he knew, he must have known – that he was never let out of sight by the Thai Special Branch. I had trouble in keeping out of their way; it meant a lot of long-distance surveillance with the field-glasses (this was why I had asked Loman for a pair) and it meant giving the little Toyota the gun on a cold engine when Kuo came out of somewhere after a couple of hours' stay. It meant risking, time after time, losing him altogether.

There was no particular travel-pattern emerging; his excursions were haphazard and his timing flexible. He made vague sight-seeing tours of the city: a motorboat trip along the Chao Phraya and the market canals, a look at the Monastery of the Dawn and the Emerald Buddha in the Wat Phra Keo. He was doing the rounds, taking his time, enjoying himself while I had to sit with the A.O. Jupiters focused at a hundred yards and one foot over the clutch, one hand on the starter-switch, the gear already in, one eye on the mirror so that I didn't smash someone up if I had to take two seconds to get out of a parking-gap it had taken twenty minutes to find. One morning I had to spend over an hour watching them grab the king cobras and squeeze the venom out of their fangs at the Pasteur snake-farm because Kuo was so interested.

The only reward I had was the certain knowledge that Kuo was behaving out of character. He was *in* character as a tourist; but he wasn't a tourist. He'd been in this city before. (He is still reported as having been in Bangkok on 9 June 1946, when King Ananda was found shot dead with a revolver near his body. Suicide has never been established and that verdict is still un-acceptable to certain members of the Royal Household.)

During the six days of Kuo's sightseeing tour the only incident came when he stopped his Hino Contessa 1300 for too long outside the Royal Palace at the main Sanam Chai Road gates. Four men in neat suits got out of the car that had pulled up behind his and spoke to him through the window. Then they got him out of his car and put him in theirs, driving off. I had to wait two hours outside Phra Ratchawang police-station near the river before I could pick up the tag. The information filtered to me through Loman the next day: they'd grilled him, searched him and taken the film from his camera.

This was an unnecessary move. He had known they'd been shadowing him and they didn't have to show their hand. Nor could they have hoped to find any excuse for either keeping him under the key or escorting him across the frontier. They could have done that anyway without an excuse. Their very evident object was to let him run loose and keep him in sight and hope he would set up the machinery for a kill on the 29th, and then scotch it at the fifty-ninth second so that he couldn't make a break and set up a reserve operation.

This was my object too but I couldn't see why they'd shown their hand. The snatch outside the Palace was the equivalent of my going up to him on the steps of the Royal Thai Athletic Association gymnasium and telling him that if he didn't watch out I was going to tread on his face. There was no point. The only thing I could suppose was that the patrol crew had panicked, seeing a professional sitting in the dim interior of a car parked within easy range of the open windows of the Palace, and had roughed him up a little to justify their interest in him.

They couldn't have been serious about it. Two of the known internationals – Zotta and Vincent – never openly cross a frontier into the country where they have a killing to do; sometimes they are never seen in the country at all; it is only the manner and pattern of the killing that identifies them, much too late. But Kuo has style and will wave his passport at the immigration officers on his way in; perhaps he likes the fuss it causes; perhaps he likes it that whenever he crosses a frontier the life of the president is immediately assumed to be in hazard, though ninety per cent of his journeys are made simply to watch the Olympic Games or take in a world-championship fight.

If they had been serious about him this time they could have fixed the interrogation at Phra Ratchawant police-station and got him out of the country. They didn't want to do that – didn't want to lose him, because he would at once cross into Thailand again incognito from Laos or Cambodia or Burma and go straight to ground. If he went to ground they might just as well shoot the target VIP themselves because the outcome would now be certain: Kuo would hole up only if he had business to do.

So they had probably panicked. It wasn't pleasant for them. With orders from the highest source to ensure safety they were watching a known professional assassin touring their city at a time when coloured lanterns were being strung across the bridges and flags were going up across the façade of almost every building in readiness to greet a most important visitor in thirteen days from now.

I thought of contacting Loman to ask one question: *had* they in fact panicked or were they changing their tactics? He might not even be able to find out. We had no liaison. We didn't exist. They would have to make their own plan; we would make ours.

At one point Kuo came out of a restaurant and I was blocked in by a solid jam of traffic for five or six minutes. I had to baulk an ambulance and take a one-way street in the wrong direction, clearing two blocks and cutting across the end of the street where Kuo was pointed, before I could back-track in a square series and get behind him. I must have caned the Toyota to the limit. Would it amuse Control if I sent a signal tonight? *Am slowly wrecking Compact Hire machine. Suggest a discreet cheque for damage due to misuse be tendered to them on surrendering vehicle.*

On the sixth day I managed to get a city paper and read some of it while Kuo was in the Turkish Baths in Sukhumvit Soi 21.

A second wave of arrests by the Bangkok Metropolitan Police Command had rounded up more than five hundred suspects and stolen property valued at some ninety thousand *baht* had been seized. It was referred to as a 'drive against crime' and there was no mention of any action against subversives or political undercover agents. The front page reported 'considerable difficulty' being encountered in choosing the best itinerary for the motorcade through the city on the 29th of the month. (It was the first public announcement that the actual tour would take place on the day of the Person's arrival.)

Loman had told me that the exact itinerary would be kept

secret until as late as possible and that at least five routes would be announced during the few days prior to the tour so that no one could get a solid fix on it.

There was nothing else in the paper about the threat (the receipt of it in London had been reported by the Bangkok Press ten days ago but had since been played down), so I took out the Kuo travel-pattern I had logged and tried to read some kind of significance into it again. Certainly there were pointers but they didn't add up to much: five visits to Wat Phra Keo (the Royal Chapel) three to the Lumpini polo grounds, three to the Pasteur snake-farm, two trips along the river by motor-launch (privately hired) and one half-hour stop in the car-park on the new Link Road parallel with Rama IV. Only the Chapel and the Lumpini visits had any bearing: the Chapel was close to the Royal Palace and a polo game had been arranged for the 30th.

Among several one-shot visits in Kuo's pattern were Government House (almost certain to be on the final itinerary of the motorcade), the James Thompson Thai Art Exhibition (almost certain to be a stopping-off point) and the Phra Chula Chedi, a temple overlooking the Link Road near Rama IV.

There was only this one relationship in the whole pattern: the temple and the new road.

I had begun resenting the police shadows. They could take it in shifts and I was on what amounted to a 24-hour tour of duty – six days of it so far – with biscuit-crumbs trodden into the floor of the Toyota because there was no chance of proper meals and a jaded reflection in the windscreen under the street-lamps because there hadn't been time for more than snatched intervals of sleep. The work was more difficult because I had to keep clear of the police patrols and still hold the tag on Kuo, and since they were tagging him too it took a lot of doing. Loman had been firm on this: the Director General of the Police Department knew we were operating but had made it clear that if we got in the way we'd be told to pull out.

I didn't know how much power Loman had as the director of the only agent in the field. If pushed (that is, if the police decided to warn me off), I believed he could stir up London, but it might mean official telegrams from Ambassador to Foreign Secretary to cover unofficial requests and permissions and we didn't have time for that. I had one single preliminary mission: *to keep Kuo in sight.* To tag him till his travel-pattern showed significance or until he made a move that would give us a clue to his intentions. The mission Loman had first handed me – to 'arrange for the assassination' – had been dealt with as we went along. After three days of tagging Kuo I had drawn up two foolproof alternative set-ups for a long-distance shot and given them to Loman. I had selected those streets that were nearly certain to be on the itinerary: they were major roads in the area of a triangle formed by the Royal Palace, the British Embassy and Lumpini Park. One set-up included the Phra Chula Chedi temple and the Link Road.

Twice Loman had brought me to the point of a brawl. He had used the same polished Junior Conservative Society phrase each time: 'I needn't impress on you the fully urgent necessity of keeping Kuo in sight.' The first time I had diluted the adrenalin with a quick drink and the second time I had said: 'Look, I've been keeping myself alive for five days on a gutful of biscuits and something like a dozen hours of sleep and I've torn the tyres off the Toyota and changed it for a new one, so if you think I'm not impressed with the fully urgent necessity of keeping that bastard in sight you must be off your bloody head.'

He gave a smooth smile and said that he expected I felt better now. I probably did. I wouldn't have minded so much if he wasn't always so beautifully shaven: I'd been keeping the stubble down by quick jabs with a clockwork thing in the car.

On the evening of the sixth day Kuo and his two bodyguards went into the Lotus Bar in the Indo-Chinese quarter not long after seven o'clock. I took the chance and stretched my legs, noting a police-car standing off and the two-man shadow patrol taking up station on the far side of the bar. We were comfortably within habitual patterns: Kuo always picked somewhere to drink at this hour and stayed for an average of thirty minutes; then he would go somewhere else to dine. The thirty minutes took us to seven-forty. By seven-fifty-five I was back in the car and fretting a bit and by eight-fifteen I was worried. At eight-thirty I got out of the car and crossed the road and went into the bar and he wasn't there.

Kuo had gone to ground.

Chapter Six

BLANK

So I had learned him and lived with him until I knew him as I would know a brother, and now in a strange and terrible way I missed him. He had always been there in the intimate round window of the 8 × 60 Jupiters and now it was blank.

I went on working until midnight, taking a trajectory across the town from the Lotus Bar to the Résidence Florale (where he had an apartment) to the Thai Room at the Plaza (where he always had Peking Duck) to Nick's No. 1 and the Shangrilla and the Sbai-thong in Rajprasong and the Roulette Room at the Vendôme. And he wasn't in any of them. His two favourite *maisons privées*. Blank. The opium house near the Phra Chao. Blank. The hermaphrodite show at the Emerald Gate. Blank. All the way to midnight, drawing blank.

Loman was waiting for me in my room at the Pakchong – I had signalled the safe-house, fully urgent.

He took it very well.

'The police lost him too, and they were in strength. It was a very difficult assignment, very.'

He didn't look so well groomed tonight. Bags under the eyes. I asked: 'What are they doing about it?'

'Very little, oddly enough. Kuo isn't their chief interest. The last wave of arrests brought in a well-organized subversive group under orders from Peking. They think the real danger was there. They think one of their number defected recently and sent the threat to London. They're working on it now with some of our security people giving them a hand – after all, *we* hold the actual written evidence.'

I knew why he said that. Security were having trouble with Thai Home Office; there were too many of them, a good half-dozen. The written evidence of the threat was their only card.

'Doesn't your air-conditioner work?' Loman wanted to know. His pink skin was gleaming.

'I told them to switch it off. All day in the heat of the street and a few hours up here with that thing on and you've got pneu-

40

monia.' I sounded like an old man fretting about his health.
'Then what *are* they doing about Kuo? Nothing?'

'Routine search, of course.'

'They won't find him that way.'

'How will they find him?' He was standing in the middle of the room looking me hard in the eyes. He wasn't sure of me, not sure how seriously I was taking this thing.

'By keeping out of my way. And out of *his* way. I don't know if the Kuo cell is on to me. I've worked in strict hush for six days but then I had to show my hand, combing the town – the Lotus Bar and all the other places. But if they're *not* on to me I've still got a chance. I know the whole cell now – two bodyguards and four operatives. He works with a team like a matador with a *cuadrilla*, always has. I can recognize any one of them and, God knows, I can recognize Kuo. If the police lay off they'll show themselves sooner or later; then it's a question of time.'

'Thirteen days.'

He was standing there sweating like a pig.

'I want you to know something, Loman. This job didn't appeal to me when it was sprung on me cold but I finally took it on and now I'm in deep and I'm not backing out. I know what's happened. I've lost the adverse party and he's gone to ground and nothing can stop him setting up the kill. The Person isn't safe any more. Don't think it doesn't mean anything to me.'

I was too tired to think of the right words but he must have caught the tone because he drew a breath and nodded.

'I'm quite sure you realize the extreme gravity of the situation.'

For the first time I felt sorry for the poor bastard. Even his bow tie wasn't straight. He wished he'd never roped in the Bureau and he wished he'd never chosen me for the running-boy and now it was a bit too late to do anything about it.

I turned away from him and looked down from the open windows, the only open windows in the whole hotel. The air was like cotton-wool against the skin. The street was still sliding past in a gold stream down there, bumper to bumper, coloured lanterns flowering right across the park, a pulse of way-out Occidental rhythms rising from late-night garden rooms, people dancing under the lights, under the leaves. No one wanted to sleep.

'How is it going,' I asked him, 'in Room 6?'

'Everyone is very occupied, of course.' His pedantic phrases sounded thin now, running on like a ticker-tape oblivious to the crash it was announcing. 'The Ambassador takes the chair himself when he can. There are continual telegrams exchanged with London but they mostly concern the security situation as such – '

'Does the FO know what we're doing?'

'I can't say, of course. All I can do is send our own regular signals and leave it to Control whether or not to inform the Minister. The first confidential press conference was held yesterday – '

'Christ,' I said.

'I realize that's a contradiction in terms, but they *are* being co-operative and of course we don't have to give them everything – they have been given nothing about *us*. I don't like press conferences at a time like this, don't like them at all. One has to show that one isn't – erm – '

'Screaming with fright.'

'That one isn't *worried*. Yes.'

I stared down at the flow of lights, mesmerized, a sleepy calm creeping over the jangle of my nerves, the music from the leafy gardens stifling my own inner scream of fright. It was time to shut everything down.

'What are your immediate plans?' he was asking me, coming towards the windows.

'Sleep,' I said. 'For twelve hours. And God help anyone who tries to stop me.'

The Maltz system of psycho-cybernetics breaks new ground in that it likens the subconscious to a computer to which the forebrain submits problems for resolution. Some of its concepts derive from accepted disciplines including that of the sleep processes.

The dreams I experienced during the next twelve hours were variations on the same dominant theme, and the only clear memory of them was summarized in a repetition of what Loman had told me a week ago:

You now have information that a man revered in his own country and respected abroad is going to have the guts to expose himself to a threat of death because he won't refuse his duty. You also know that if the very elaborate machinery for his protection breaks down and if this valuable life is lost because of your own petty feelings against me as your director in the field, it's going to be your fault – your fault alone. And you won't be able to live with it.

The data was fed to the computer in the form of images: the Person, hands tucked behind him, eyes quizzical – a quick laugh as he got the point an instant before the others, a tilt of his chin as he turned and moved on beside his companion. And Kuo: strong, short-bodied and well-tailored, placing his feet with deliberation, his Asiatic features made half anonymous by the smoked glasses. And Loman: smoothly shaven, the mind cold behind the hard bright stare.

The images merged as the computer collated the data: Kuo with his deliberate steps taking him past the shop window where the photograph looked out with quizzical eyes – and suddenly the crowds and the flags and the flowers and the cross-hairs of the telescopic sight bearing on the moving target and the crash of the shot with Loman's face distorted by the long-drawn-out scream of fright. The kill.

It's going to be your fault – your fault alone.

The data wasn't new; it had been going into the computer since the day I had accepted the mission; but in sleep there were no distractions and the subconscious was totally engaged.

The sleep-curves had shallowed out by noon of the next day and I woke and spent an hour getting clean and drinking coffee and thinking about nothing. Then I began looking for Kuo.

The streets were more festive every day and there were flags everywhere, and flowers. People began cheering the Ambassador's car when they saw the standard. The florists along Plern Chit Road competed with one another, making immense displays round the gold-framed photograph – red and white flowers, blue ribbons.

I was a spectre at the feast, haunting the streets, the stubble growing again, the Toyota taking me through the city in a maze of my own making and spinning out a travel-pattern that somewhere and sometime must coincide with his.

Loman wanted me to make contact every day but I kept clear of him when I could because there was nothing to report. On the sixth day of the hunt he intercepted me in the lobby of the Pakchong.

'I may have to tell London to advise the Minister,' he said.

I stood looking at him, aching for sleep.

He said: 'We have five days more. I've tried to convince Police-colonel Ramin that we are on to the biggest danger – Kuo. It's a case for a dragnet. He won't hear of it.'

'He was keen enough before. Never left the bastard alone.'

'Ramin believes the only danger was from the subversive group he rounded up. He's already taking credit for having cleared the city. There are rumours that Kuo has left Thailand.'

'Naturally. He's circulating them himself.'

He asked me: 'What do you think of your chances?'

'It's a question of time. I told you before. If the police have stopped looking it's a help – I've got a clear field.'

'The Person is due here in five days and – '

'You don't have to keep – '

'I'm not just rubbing it in – don't misunderstand me. I mean simply that the visit can't be called off at the last minute. It's a very big affair. There has to be time to announce the diplomatic cold. At least two days. So we have three days left – it's no longer practical to call it five.'

I thought he'd begun swaying on his feet but the trellis archway into the fountain court was swaying too.

'All right. Three.'

'I would like you to report daily from now on.

'I'll report.'

He nodded. 'You need some sleep now.'

'How did you know?' I said, and went up the stairs, leaving him standing there.

It was no go the next day. I took long loops through the city, checking and rechecking the points where the Kuo cell had shown itself, finding myself again and again in the temple and Link Road area. It was the psycho-cybernetic computer sending me there, correcting my course with negative-feedback data. It had the answer. The Pra Chula Chedi. Perhaps it was right. I didn't know.

For the third time I drove out to the airport across the unending rice-fields, vetting the few buildings and trying to arrange a set-up that Kuo might use if he meant to kill early and make sure of it before the security net could stop him. There were only a dozen or so buildings that would allow less than a 90° shot, and only two of these were placed on a curve in the road or at an angle that would bring a car head-on in the sights.

The airport looked very gay, decked out with flowers filling the main terrace. It looked welcoming. I wondered whether he would come, and if he came, whether he would live.

The duotone Chevrolet in the main parking area was moving forward as I turned towards the gates and I suddenly got fed up and made a quick full-circle and forced it to a stop against the fence. I left my own car and climbed into the back of hers. She just sat there, not turning her head but giving me her steady direct gaze in the mirror as I said:

'I want to know what you're doing here and why you've had me tagged for the last fifteen days. Just straight answers, beginning now.'

Chapter Seven

THE RITUAL

'There's nothing,' she said, 'that I can tell you.'

I had been leaning forward. Now I slid back and rested my head on the rear squab, my half-closed eyes on the mirror where hers watched me. It was a big car, comfortable. It would be nice to be driven somewhere, along a road that ran straight and had no danger-spots, no traps.

The airport was suddenly aglow with light as the dusk fell. The flowers became vivid.

'What is your name?' I asked.

'Maine.'

'All of it.'

'Vinia Maine.'

She turned her lean body and laid one arm along the back of her seat and looked at me directly instead of in the mirror. There wasn't any expression in the wide clear eyes; they were just alert.

I said: 'It doesn't sound very likely. Your cover-name, is it?'

She said nothing.

'Who were the tags? The thin one, and the one with the splay-footed walk. Who were they?'

The vivid flowers were reflected in her eyes.

'Who were they?'

I watched the pulse beating in her slim throat. She didn't look away from me.

'Where are they now? Why are you having to do their job? Why did you tag me here?'

Her lips parted. A second's hesitation. Then: 'I thought you might be getting on a plane.'

Her voice was low and its clear timbre made my drowsiness worse. It was a voice to send a child to sleep.

'What would you have done,' I asked her, 'if I'd got on a plane?'

'It would have depended where you were going.'

'Oh, come on – come on!' I was suddenly sitting up straight.

Loman was a *hell* of an intelligence director if he couldn't keep this bitch out of my way – I'd told him to, I'd made a point of it. 'Just give me basic answers, will you? Where d'you *think* I might have been going in a plane?'

'Into China.'

'What would you have done?'

'Stopped you.'

'How?'

'By warning you.'

'Warning me?'

'By telling you why you can't cross into China.'

'I'm taking the Midnight so tell me now.'

The smile was tentative, starting in the eyes and then touching the mouth. 'No. You're not.'

I looked away from her through the window. A car had come into the parking area, a taxi. I watched the people get out.

She said: 'I came alone. There was no time to tell anyone where I was going.'

I looked back at her. For an instant, because I was tired and because the big car was comfortable, I wondered what had happened to the left side of her face.

'What outfit are you in?' I asked. 'You and the two tags? Security? Why can't you do your job on your own instead of following me about like pilot-fish hanging on for the pickings? I've lost the bastard – you know that. But I'm going to find him and when I find him you won't be there. By God, I'll make sure of that.' I opened the door. 'Tell them to lay off. Keep out of my way. I don't like hangers-on.'

I got out and slammed the door. The driving-window was open and I leaned in and jerked the ignition-key out and threw it across the flower-beds.

'If you have to cross into China,' she said looking up at me intently, 'please see me first. I can always be contacted at the Embassy.'

'You won't see me again.'

I got into the Toyota.

At noon the next day I reported to Loman at the safe-house in Soi Suek 3. He didn't ask if I'd made any progress because he knew I'd be only too damned glad to tell him if I had.

'That bitch at the Embassy,' I said. 'Who is she?'

He said curiously: 'That's the second time you've mentioned her.'

'I told you to keep her out of my way. She tagged me last night and she's had me tagged for the past fifteen days – who the hell are they?'

After a bit he said: 'I'll try to find out. It's the secretary to the Cultural Attaché you mean, is it?'

'Scarface.'

'I've had no information on her, of course.'

It was never possible to tell when he was lying. In his game it was one of his assets. I let it go. He talked for a bit to see if he could glean anything from my mood. He would have given a lot just for one crumb, one small crumb of hope. Before I left him I said:

'All right – I've got two more days.'

I went straight back to the Pakchong and had my two cases sent down to the car. It looked as though Loman didn't know who she was or why she was hanging on so I would just have to fade. Occasionally you get a fool girl with a built-in do-it-yourself Mata-Hari kit in her wig and they play hell all over the departments picking bus-tickets out of the w.p.b. and sending them to Codes and Ciphers. This was one of them. They lived in their own cold-war dream-world and talked out of the sides of their mouths – 'Don't cross into China' – that sort of thing. This one had roped in a couple of clerks from the Cultural Aid for Distressed Pomeranian Pavement-artists and put them on to my track, in between cosy bedtimes.

I spent ten minutes in the thick of the city with both eyes on the mirror and jabbing the Toyota heel-and-toe through the corners to shake off any possible tag, then made a straight line for a safe hotel near the Pan-Am office. I had used it before and the management was still the same.

Then I worked till midnight and drew blank.

There was a message from Loman the next day: Pangsapa was trying to contact me. It took an hour to find him but I didn't lose patience; if he had information on Kuo it was worth a whole day. He was supervising a shipment at one of his wharves along the Chao Phraya and I had to wait until he had given orders for his overseer to take charge.

'We will go into my office,' he lisped. 'You will have some tea, I hope?'

'There's no time, Pangsapa.' Tea in this latitude meant a protracted ceremony.

He wore Western clothes today and his office was functional in design so that our meeting had the appearance of the mundane, as if a householder were taking out a mortgage with the help of life assurance. Except that looking into these quiet yellow eyes I remembered the beautiful fish.

'I understand,' he said considerately. 'People tell me that your time is very short, and very limited. I wish I could be of some further use. That's why I hoped you might come to see me.'

He had the manner of a bargainer and I tried mentally to put a price on his information – if he had any and if it would lead me to Kuo. But there were the imponderables: even if I found Kuo it wasn't certain that I could stop him making his kill. How much would the Bureau go to, with the life of the Person in hazard?

There was no time for bargaining. They'd have to pay what it said on the ticket.

'Let's use short words, Pangsapa. You wanted to see me and I'm here.'

He nodded. 'Very well. I'll be brief. First, I've no information for you. I don't know where he is. But I would like to help you find him before it's too late. That might expose me – or friends whom I cherish – to some danger.' He got up from his desk and looked from the big low window. The shadow of a crane swung across him. I believed him to be genuinely interested in the loading of his shipment and I cursed him for not being as interested in Kuo. 'You see,' he said, without turning from the window, 'I don't know much about you, Mr Quiller. I don't know how dangerous your work is, or to what degree I and my friends would share your dangers if we took' – he swung his head and looked straight at me – 'exceptional measures to help you.'

I said: 'It's no go. I'm on a mission – you know that. And you know what it is. There's nothing I can add.'

His wistful smile appeared. 'If you want me to help you find this man it would be natural for me to ask you more about your mission. After all, they are practically the same thing. But I

49

won't press you. Just tell me about yourself, as distinct from your present work.'

I leaned forward and cupped my face in my hands. The light from the big window burned my eyes.

'Particularize,' I said.

I heard him sitting down again.

'Are all your missions dangerous, Mr Quiller?'

'I'd be safer in bed.' It was all my subconscious could think about. Sleep.

'Do you always work in an official capacity?'

'There's an office behind my work, just as there's an office behind the work of shipping snow.' A bit impolite. To hell. He had *no* bloody information.

'Does the Government reward you sufficiently for the dangers you're asked to face?'

God knows I'd asked him to use short words but this was getting basic. I said:

'Make me an offer, and tell me for what.' I emerged from my hands because I needed to watch him now.

'You mustn't misunderstand me,' he said quickly. 'It's so difficult, you see, having to put my questions without any concession to subtlety. It makes them seem so crude. The Occidental can do it, and it has its advantages – it must save so much time at the conference tables. But "short words" are difficult currency east of the Mediterranean, so you must forgive me.' With what seemed an effort to be accommodating he leaned towards me and said: 'I'll put all my questions into one. What is your status?'

'In London?' I didn't like his drift but the only alternative to following it was to shut up; and I had to find Kuo and Pangsapa might work the trick. Tomorrow was the last day. 'You mean how important am I to the Government?'

'That would be a way of putting it, yes.'

Maybe he was just bargaining, wanting to know how much I could call on. The last time I had been good for fifty thousand *baht*.

I said: 'You've heard of Abel?'

'I have.'

'Lonsdale?'

'I have.'

'I'd say I'm about their weight.'

He nodded slowly. 'Thank you. You see, I like working with big people. I can do more for them and they can do more for me.'

I got up, annoyed with him. It was quite simple. He had impressive information sources and his network had told him that I was up against it and having a bad time trying to find Kuo, so he'd got me along to question me and assess the price. There was nothing wrong with bargaining: a value has to be set on goods; I was annoyed with him only because the deadline was so appallingly close and money wasn't important. Maybe that was because the Bureau was going to fork out, not me.

'All right, Pangsapa. If you can give me a lead on Kuo before noon tomorrow what's it going to cost?'

He came round the desk and stood as close to me as any Oriental will ever stand to his companion.

'Nothing.'

He was known to be a man who would do anything for money, unless Loman's dossier on him was duff. I asked:

'With how many noughts?'

He really took my little indiscretions remarkably well. 'You may put it down to what you called my "undying love for the monarchy" if you wish. I will tell you simply that although I have no information at present on the whereabouts of this man I will make every effort to help you find him. I may not be lucky, but I will try. And if I succeed it will cost you nothing.'

He opened the door for me and we stood on the timber balcony overlooking the dockside where the crane was still swinging. There was no point in asking him to explain and I was too tired to worry the thing so I just said:

'You can always contact me through Loman.'

I went down the steps.

The heat was worse now. The sun was turning the city to brass and it burned under the haze. The Toyota had become an oven – I couldn't always park in the shade.

That day I worked nineteen hours and I drew blank. There was no word from Pangsapa.

The next morning I tried to contact Loman by telephone at three places – his hotel, the British Embassy and the safe-house –

and had no luck. So it was at twelve noon when we met in Soi Suek 3 according to routine.

He looked knotted up with nerves and didn't even ask for my report, going straight into one of his toneless monologues.

'We held an emergency conference two hours ago in Room 6. It has now been agreed to signal London and add a recommendation that the Minister himself should be informed of the Kuo situation. The risk is quite unimaginable if we leave it any longer than – '

'I've found him,' I said.

I hadn't had time to question what had happened. It's always dangerous, on a mission, not to have time to think.

But the morning was mine. Within an hour of putting the Toyota through the routine travel-pattern I saw one of the Kuo cell coming out of the gunsmith's in New Road. It had been bound to happen: the only question was how long it would take. I had told Loman that much. Because you can't spend twenty hours a day, day after day, combing a town for a man without finding him in the end, unless he's holed up permanently. I knew that Kuo couldn't hole up permanently because he had work to do and it was work that must take him into the open.

For eight days I had been following the established Kuo pattern and keeping watch on every single place where he had ever showed himself. The entire pattern had been committed to my memory, beginning with his points of call that I had checked in the few hours after losing him in the Lotus Bar – *Low Flora ties Nick by thongs angrily to emigrate* . . . Lotus Bar, Résidence Florale, Thai Room, Nick's No. 1, Sbaithong, Shangrilla, Emerald Gate . . . There were some thirty-odd places and I had mentally listed them in descending order of priority. At the top of that list was the Temple–Link Road sector. My instincts homed strongly on that area and I knew why. The Maltz psycho-cybernetic mechanism kept sending me back there. There was also a second reason.

The man in the Kuo cell had a taxi waiting for him near the gunsmith's and I put a tag on him that it was impossible for him to flush, simply because I couldn't afford to let him go. At noon I would have to report to Loman and this was the day of the deadline.

52

I think I have never tagged a man so mercilessly well. He never knew I was there. He led me straight to an apartment block on the river side of the city and I was still there at the kerb in the Toyota half an hour later when Kuo came out with his two bodyguards and got into a car. He got in first and the two men handed him, very carefully, a roll of gold cloth.

The temptation to throw blind was strong: to hang back and let them go, remove all risk of their sensing me; to take the series of tacking short-cuts that would get me there before them and give me time to climb the stairs of the Botanical Museum. But there was a greater risk: that they were going somewhere else, somewhere I didn't know about.

In the end it was a compromise. After ten minutes the Kuo driver sensed me and began square-turns, block after block, playing the lights on the amber and using his speed through Lumpini Park. It was no go. He would never lead me anywhere useful now that he knew I was there in his mirror. Kuo would order him to keep on driving until he flushed me however long it took.

So I dropped back, putting up a fair show of being baulked by the traffic at the angle of Sukumvit and Rama IV and making a couple of feints and turning *back* up Sukumvit into Dheb Prasit Lane and into Rama IV and speeding up dead straight and due west towards Lumpini, working on a seventy-thirty chance. It was all I had.

They didn't come into the mirror. The Botanical Museum was in the Link Road area and I left the Toyota in the driveway and took the field-glasses with me.

At the Museum there is a staircase at one side with a small window on each landing. I had been there more than once in the last eight days, going up to the reading-room on the top floor so that the girl at the desk in the main hall wouldn't hear my footsteps halt at the third landing and wonder why (the place echoed a lot), then coming quietly down to the small window that overlooked the Phra Chula Chedi, the Temple on the Link Road.

They came within minutes. I focused the Jupiters.

One of them – not Kuo – got out of the car and went through the temple gardens, coming back with a man in a yellow robe,

53

a priest. He leaned at the window of the car; in the 8 × 60 lens I could see his lips moving. Then he straightened up and they handed him the roll of gold cloth. He carried it with reverence through the temple gardens and the car drove away.

I am not easily moved to repugnance, but it was the ritual that was so ugly, the ritual.

Chapter Eight

DIABOLUS

The whole thing nearly came unstuck.

It was typical of our relationship: we'd known from the beginning that we weren't going to get on together; we'd known also that somehow we would have to. But this time it wasn't personal; it was on a question of policy.

'I can't sanction it.' That was his first reaction.

He spent most of the time walking about and I had to suffer his long silences while he stopped to stare at the rosewood buddha and the moonstone and the Pan-Orient Jewel Company calendar on the wall.

'I cannot see *how* I could sanction it.'

After a bit I just sat down and shut my eyes except when he came up to talk to me. Even then he was talking half the time to himself, playing it aloud, trying to get a grip on it. I was hard up for sleep and would have dozed off in the chair if I hadn't been sitting on a bomb.

'It is the most *sensitive* operation I have ever been presented with.'

I could hear by his footsteps that he was standing in front of me again so I opened my eyes and said:

'You asked me for a set-up. It's the only one that can work. There are plenty of others but they're all chancy. You've thought of them and I've thought of them and there's something wrong with all of them except this one so don't let's waste time going over – '

'*Everything* is wrong with *this* one.'

'And everything is right.'

I sat watching him struggle. Certainly there was a lot to this operation that would put the fear of Christ into a seasoned agent – the whole set-up was pivoted on a needle-point. But it had advantages, big ones, bigger than any of the other plans could give us. He wanted to launch it; he would give a great deal to see it run; he was an intelligence director of long experience and this thing excited him, fascinated him. It was sensitive and it was elegant. What he was doing, as he shifted about and stared at things he didn't see, was trying to talk himself into saying yes.

I let him struggle with it while I sat there with thoughts of my own. I had already made my decision: if he agreed to directing this operation I would set it up and push through with it win or lose. If he couldn't sanction it I would sign off the mission and get out of Bangkok. No half-measures: if he tried to talk me into one of the other plans it was no go.

The second reason (the first was the Maltz mechanism) for the strong homing of my instincts on the temple near the Link Road was that it was one of the alternative set-ups I had given Loman some time ago. It was the feature of one of the 'assassination arrangements' he had first asked me for. The Phra Chula Chedi, with its white frescoed walls and golden tower and beautiful gardens, was a perfect vantage-point for Kuo. It was a gun-site commanding the whole length of the Link Road.

It was to the temple that Kuo himself had taken the roll of gold cloth, consigning it to the safe keeping of the man garbed as a priest. There had been people about, passing along the pavement. It didn't matter. Gold cloth – tapestries, sacred draperies – were common enough in the city temples. This roll had been something over three feet long and its weight – judging by the way they had handled it – had been ten or twelve pounds. Gold fibre is heavy: the cloth itself would weigh in the region of five or six pounds.

It didn't matter that the passers-by had seen it. In another way, it did. It was Kuo's hallmark: stylishness. He had taken a braggart pleasure in bringing to this sacred place, in view of the people of this city, the instrument of Cain that would send this city – and all England – into mourning.

The thing had been done with the semblance of a ritual. Kuo the Mongolian was a man short in the body and with a deliberate gait, his face disguised by smoked glasses; but he would be more accurately described as a man who would do this thing in this way. This was his whole character expressed in one gesture. He was Diabolus.

So Loman's misgivings didn't count with me.

He was standing over my chair again and I opened my eyes. He said almost pettishly: 'You know perfectly well that in any case I can't sanction homicide.'

'I'm not asking you to.'

'But the entire operation hinges on – '

'For God's sake, Loman, we're wasting time.' I got out of the chair, fed up with him. 'One of them's going to die, isn't he? Which d'you want it to be?'

He started pacing up and down again till I stopped him and made him talk and go on talking. In half an hour we reached a deadlock and it took another half an hour to break it. Talking that helped him, helped us both. We were getting used to the operation and it didn't scare us any more.

'We are always up against the same difficulty, Quiller. Lack of peripheral support. We haven't any junior agents to do the general background work – tagging, guarding, manning a courier line. All chiefs and no Indians. That's why you lost Kuo at the Lotus Bar – we didn't have a man on the other exit. We can't ask for assistance from any police department – as I've told you, Colonel Ramin will have nothing to do with me. For this reason we have very little information. Plenty of raw intelligence but nobody who can analyse it for us and give us a complete picture. Therefore we know practically nothing of what plans the Bangkok Metropolitan people have in mind – or even what our own security is doing. Their responsibility is very high and they're jealous of it.' He took a couple of turns and came back, giving me a hard bright stare. 'By which I mean that if we launch this operation we shall be on our own. Entirely on our own.'

I said: 'It's the only way I can work. You know that.' I had to cede him this point. The mission suited me but it didn't suit him: he specialized in operations with a well-organized cell, established access and first-class communications. This wasn't in his field. It hadn't been in mine until the Kuo pattern had shown me the way in.

There was no point now in telling Loman that he had roped in the Bureau and me with it and that it was his own responsibility. He had to be sold my operation by positive, not negative, argument. I told him:

'Lack of peripheral support isn't a difficulty in this case. It's because we're on our own that we can work as we like. We're responsible to Control for results and the dreams don't count. No one is responsible to *us* – there aren't any junior agents to get caught in the blast when we light the fuse. That's the whole idea about the Bureau, isn't it? You've said it yourself: we don't exist. It lets us do things that no other department can do.' I stood close to him. 'You can't lose, Loman. With a bit of luck and some good organization the security people sent out with the Person are going to give him all the protection he needs. If they can't stop Kuo then the local networks will – the Thai Home Office, Special Branch and Metro Police. With luck. But if he gets through them all . . . and if all the luck runs out . . . we'll be there, you and I, plugging the hole.' We stood so close that I could see my own reflection in his hard bright eyes. I needed to do no more than murmur, 'And we can bring it off. And if we bring it off, who's going to ask how we did it? Control? Control never asks. It would never keep an agent if we had to account for our methods. So we're in the clear and we're on our own and the set-up's waiting.'

I moved away from him and gave him five seconds to think. He had to have those few seconds without my eyes on him so that he could look into himself for his own counsel – but I gave him no more than five because the final shot had to go in timed to exactitude:

'And it's a beauty . . . isn't it?'

Sensitive, elegant, simple, brutal and just. A classic. Dog eat dog.

It was absurd. He'd spent so long, before, talking me into this mission. Now I had to sell it back to him.

'What do you need?' he asked.

And I knew it was a deal.

'Three things. A base. A dark-room. A look at the car.'

'Nothing else?'

'Your general supervision. I'm out of sleep. I could make a mistake. There won't be much time for sleep. I've got your direction in any case. I'm all right, Jack – how are you?'

He asked me: 'What kind of base do you need?'

He spoke with the dulled tone of a punch-drunk. He had committed himself and had no time to think about it yet. I wished him joy in the small hours of the night.

'There's an office block at the intersection of the Link Road and Rama IV facing east with the name Taylor-Speers on a board. They're demolition contractors and the work doesn't start till the middle of next month because they're held up with their schedule: they've wrecked an electric main under the tram-terminal sheds they've just pulled down. It's a British outfit and you'll find them in the book. I want any one of the top-floor rooms at the front and no one's to know I'm there.'

He didn't like it.

'Colonel Ramin,' he said, 'tells me that the police will be checking upwards of three hundred uninhabited rooms overlooking the motorcade route on the morning of the 29th. They are already working on the lists of residents of several thousand other rooms.'

'I can deal with that. I've been in there.'

He still didn't like it.

'Taylor-Speers are bound to let their workers into the building on that day to watch the motorcade. It's been declared a national holiday and it would be natural for them to do that.'

I said: 'That's what I want fixed. No one goes into that building on the day except the police. It's a British firm and you've got a set of official credentials – pick any one. This is a big chance for Messrs Taylor-Speers to demonstrate their steadfast loyalty to the country whose ancient soil, so forth.'

'I'll do it in my own way,' he said stuffily.

'That's our motto – the means don't count.'

'What kind of dark-room do you need?'

'Nothing special. Somewhere light-proof enough to use an enlarger in the daytime. Somewhere as near the condemned building as you can find. I don't want to show myself too much in the open street.'

'Camera gear?'

'I'll choose it myself.'

'When do you want to look at the car?'

'As soon as you can fix it.'

Our voices sounded hollow. Everything we said now, every small word, took us nearer the thing we were going to do.

'I shan't waste any time,' he said.

'I know you won't.'

He went first to the door. I would wait five minutes. That was the routine. 'One thing I forgot, Loman.' He turned to look at me. 'Can you get me a guest membership card at the Rifle Club? I need a couple of hours on their thousand-yard range. We're working on a long-shot and we don't want to miss.'

Chapter Nine

THE ORIEL

Bangkok is a city whose temples have towers of gold and whose hotels rise in alabaster from emerald palms. Here fountains play in marbled courts and women walk in silk with jewelled hair; the air is heavy with the perfumes of all Araby. It is a paradise expressly fashioned for the beguilement of princes; by day the sun spills rose light along private paths and the blue of night is webbed about with music.

The tramp was curled up on his sleeping-mat in the corner of the dusty floor where flakes of plaster fell softly from the walls with a dead-moth flutter. There was a smell of mildew in the air: water from the last rains had leaked from fissures in the roof, and was rotting the ceiling battens. It would never dry out; the hammers would be here first, felling the whole edifice like a beast in the *abattoir*.

Loman had worked fast, I'll say that for him. Taylor-Speers had rallied to the flag and this rotting hulk was my lair for the last of its days. The ghost had moved in early, his nose quick for the smell of death.

Sometimes I slept but waked often on a thought that had to be examined. (Who was she, and was it important to know? Was there a *parallel* operation mounted, by Mil. 6 or some other group? If so it couldn't be by coincidence. By what, then? What design?'

Loman had also found me a dark-room in the next block and I had permission to use it as required. He had even convinced the Palace Security of his bona fides and we had been fetched in a police-car. Our papers were checked by guards at two points in the private grounds before we reached the royal garages.

It was an interesting vehicle: a Cadillac Fleetwood Eldorado in ivory white with gold metal fittings and amber hide. The 340 h.p. engine could push the 2-ton gross weight to 120 m.p.h. The coachwork had been converted to provide six seats, two of them folding into the mid-squab, the main rear seat being raised 9 inches for a better view. Four aerials gave radio linking with outriders and the command security vehicle. Steel-reinforced side-platforms dressed with ribbed white rubber provided foothold for a guard if he had to perform his prime duty – that of getting his body between the bullet and the man he was protecting. Special equipment included a built-in police siren, emergency lights, fire-bottles, medical kit and bullet-proof tyres.

There were five dismountable roof sections, one of sheet steel, four of bullet-proof transparent plastic.

I had told Loman: 'It's important to know which sections are going to be mounted – if any.'

'That may be difficult. It's nobody's particular decision. Our security people and Thai Security will ask for all the plastic sections to be put up. The Person himself will opt to dispense with all of them, because that is his character. Prince Udom will be in the car with him and the Palace directive is almost certain. Nobody here wants it to be demonstrated that one can travel safely through Bangkok only by virtue of bullet-proof shields.'

'Find out what you can, that's all I ask.'

It was important. These shields formed part of a pattern that comprised a lot of factors: distance, trajectory, trigonometry, ballistics. Take one shield away and it would affect the whole set-up. It could even shift the location of the sniping-post. And we had to work on the premise that whatever we knew, Kuo could find out.

Kuo wasn't just a thug with a gun for hire. He wouldn't be in the crowd at the edge of the route hoping to get in a chance shot and run before they lynched him. Hope and chance weren't in his reckoning: he was a professional. In a way he was like Loman: he worked best with a disciplined cell and good communications. Since Kuo had come to this city he had been directing his cell with precision and they would have gone out hard for information. They had to know the defence pattern and they had to find its weaknesses. They had to break it before they could kill.

Assume they know everything. Everything.

Except that I am where I am, curled on the floor like a dog in its den, waiting the chance to eat dog.

$135 \times 2 \times 8 = 2160$.

The tilt of the planet itself was a factor.

Framed in the window of my small high room was the Phra

Chula Chedi, magnificent in the morning sun. The walls were white and had no apertures except for the immense golden doors half-seen among the temple gardens. Above the walls rose the dome in a half-globe of shimmering gold, supporting the slender tower. Between dome and tower was a ring of small unglazed openings, and only from these oriels could a marksman sight the Link Road.

At a range of some two hundred yards I could look directly into them at eye-level – but it was summer and the sun was high and they were at all hours in shadow. The field-glasses couldn't beat this light-factor. No optical lens of whatever magnification could define detail inside the ring of oriels. It could be done only with a camera.

A camera, set for time-exposure, can produce a detailed image of a room so dark that objects in it are barely visible to the human eye. The camera is a light-gathering device.

The place Loman had found for me in the next block didn't sell much equipment because they were mainly in business for processing and the highest magnification they could offer was × 12. There was a shop half a mile down Rama IV but I was holed up and I didn't want to show myself in the street more than I had to. They let me take my pick from what they had on the shelves and I came up with a compromise: a Pentax X-15 25 mm single reflex with a 135 mm lens that took a × 2 Auto teleconverter and a stock adapter for my Jupiters. This 135 × 2 × 8 (lens *plus* converter *plus* field-glasses) gave a total focal length of 2160 mm and a magnification of × 16.

I set it up on a tripod with a turret-mounting that was rigid enough for the weight, but the building was old and the traffic would cause vibration so I played safe with a Pan Plus-X, 36 frames. The depth of field wasn't critical because seen through the Jupiters the wall inside the middle oriel appeared to be less than six feet back from the aperture. To cut through the heat-haze I used an H4 Vivo yellow filter; to mask out the glare of the gold dome a makeshift hood was essential and I had brought one of the three-foot cardboard cylinders they had at the shop for mailing blow-ups.

The gates of the temple gardens were hidden by a cloud of magnolias and only the top half of the doorway itself was visible; the doors were some fifteen feet high and priests and worshippers would pass into the temple without my seeing them. I had therefore to concentrate on the ring of oriels.

It was two hours before movement showed there and then I ran off six frames at 1/50th, varying the aperture from $f/2.8$ to $f/11$ and using a cable-release against vibration because of the slow speed and extreme focal length.

There was further movement twice before noon and I took ten more frames, speeds from $\frac{1}{2}$ to 1/30th, same f/stops. The haze was worse now as the heat mounted in the street so I left it at that and went down to the shop and spent half an hour in the dark-room. Even the wet negs looked promising, three of the frames being sharp. It was worth staying on: I wouldn't get better than these today because of the haze. In two hours the sharpest blow-ups were hanging up to dry. Of the sixteen essays five were successful and one perfect: a head-and-shoulders pose framed in the oriel; even the shape of the smoked glasses was recognizable – rather flat at the top with the sides tapering downwards, a metal nose-piece almost level with the top of the lenses.

This one was all I needed, and from this moment came the onset of nerves. There was no doubt left. If the protection officers failed because they were too few in number, and if the Bangkok organization failed because Colonel Ramin believed wrongly that he had covered every contingency, the shot would be fired from there, from the middle oriel of the Phra Chula Chedi, a shrine to a god who held life sacred. And it would make no difference that I would afterwards present, as evidence, a portrait of Diabolus.

The onset of nerves came now because I was committed by certainty and because a rendezvous had been established between the two of us and nothing must stop my keeping it. The date was the 29th – in three days' time. The hour was not precise, but it came to a matter of seconds: there would be a period of some ten seconds in which I would have to operate.

Loman had said: 'It is the most *sensitive* operation I have ever been presented with.'

The portrait had begun curling at the bottom corners as it dried on the clips. The face looked out from the frame of the oriel, confident, authoritative. The face of a professional. I hung two more clips at the bottom and left it there; it wouldn't matter if anyone saw it but it would matter if someone took it away so I put the heat-dried negatives in my pocket and went into the street.

It took half an hour to reach the gunsmith's a mile away – three blocks on foot and checking for tags, a trishaw and another block on foot to check again – because absolute security was now essential.

I was alone and I had to stay alone and when I came to climb to the top floor of the condemned building in three days from now to keep the rendezvous no one must know I was there.

The dealer had a first class stock and I made my choice. It was a superb instrument and Kuo himself would have approved.

Chapter Ten

HUSQVARNA

The place was cavernous and light came dimly from somewhere high under the roof. It was very quiet. As soon as I came in I saw the thing in the gloom, a full-sized male of the species – a *chula* – rearing taller than a man and with livid colours streaking its head. There must have been a hundred of them in there, male and female.

I stood listening. There was no sound but the faint rush of the traffic along Rama IV, a vibration underfoot. The light had been on when I had come in and I felt it might be dangerous to look for switches and try them.

Then he came out of the shadows, his eyes brighter than the rest of him.

'It's the best I could do,' he said.

'How safe is it?'

'Safer than the gem-shop. Nobody comes in here.'

We approached each other under the vast roof, like two people meeting on a railway station, the last train gone.

'What about exits?' I wanted to know. I don't like big places. The smaller the place the quicker you can get out.

He pointed. 'One door there, another one in the far corner. I've got the keys to two of them. Here are yours.'

I took them. He hadn't done badly. The place was within three minutes' walk of the condemned building and I had reached the first door through an alley where cover was fair – several entrances and some kind of fuel-oil tank on timber props.

My eyes had grown accustomed to the gloom and I took a final look round. The kites were hung from horizontal poles in orderly rows so that even if they were set moving by a draught their fragile paper wouldn't be damaged. The male *chulas* were barbed; the female *pakpaos* had long tails and were smaller. Many had painted faces; some bore the design of a dragon. Empty crates littered the floor.

'When is the fight?' I asked Loman.

'On the first of the month. Nobody will be here to fetch him until after the motorcade.'

I'd had no time to watch the papers but there would obviously be a kite-fight organized during the Visit. Loman was being very efficient.

'Did you have any success?' he asked me, and I showed him the print.

'It's not fully dry.'

He got his pocket-lamp and the face with the smoked glasses stared back. He said:

'And you are one hundred per cent certain.'

'And I am one hundred per cent certain.'

He took a slow breath and I knew that he felt as I had when this picture had slowly appeared from the sodium thiosulphate. We were committed.

I asked him: 'What about the itinerary?'

'Nobody knows yet.'

'We've *got* to know.'

He looked up sharply because of my tone. It was going to be trickier than ever now to keep patience with each other because of nerves.

'I am watching the situation,' he said as evenly as he could. 'It is difficult, very. I have to take care not to provoke them into shutting every door on me – my efforts to interest Colonel Ramin in Kuo have already annoyed him – '

'Can't they find out at the Embassy?'

'As soon as the Ambassador knows, I shall know.'

I was nervous about two things: that there was a rendezvous and that there might not be one. 'Look,' I told him, 'either Kuo has got his information and he *knows* the route – '

'There may have been a leak – '

'A leak or his agents have been good at their job – it doesn't matter, does it? But either he knows the route or he's setting up more than one gun-post so he can use any one of them at the last minute. He might even be training his cell to man several posts at the same time so they'll be certain. So we've *got* to know.'

He gave me a minute to cool down and then said:

'What do you think? What do you *really* think?'

'All right, but there's a risk – you know that. I think he's got the information.' Because of the roll of gold cloth. Because of the ritual. If Kuo hadn't found out the exact and final itinerary the motorcade would take he wouldn't have made such a point of personally handing the weapon to the priest at the temple – that had been the act of a man who is certain of what he is doing. If he didn't know the exact route he would have been less sure of himself. It was all I had to go on: my intimate knowledge of the man and his style. But I knew him like a brother.

'From the enquiries I have made,' Loman said, 'there seems very little doubt that whatever the final route, it will include the Link Road. There are several good reasons – the new hospital is the subject of some pride in the city and the Person will want to see it; it is easier to control large crowds lining the route along the Link Road than along the section of Rama IV that's the only alternative. It is virtually certain that the itinerary will run from the Royal Palace northwards, turn east to take in the British Embassy, then south to the Lumpini polo grounds, then westwards back towards the Palace. The single major thoroughfare from Lumpini to the railway station – en route to the Palace itself – is Rama IV; and the only possible deviation from Rama IV is through the Link Road. It may be, of course, that Kuo is working on the same theory – '

'He'd be a fool not to. I agree with all your reasons but for God's sake get some definite information for me – tell the Ambassador to get off the bloody pot. What the hell is he for?'

'He is not,' Loman said with viciously quiet pauses, 'under any obligation to *us*. We do not *exist*. He knows me simply as a member of the Special Services. If I were to ask him point-blank for information he would merely tell me to liaise with the other groups – Mil. 5, Mil. 6, the Special Branch overseas unit and Security.'

'Tell him he's indirectly responsible for the safety of the Person while he's here – '

'He is *well* aware of that.' He began walking about to get rid of his frustration and his footsteps padded without echoes despite the size of the place; the big paper kites hung as thick as clothes in a crowded wardrobe and muffled the acoustics. 'The Ambassador is a worried man – a very worried man.' He stopped in front of me from time to time in case I wasn't listening. 'The situation at the Embassy is *extremely* sensitive. Quite apart from the normal rivalry between the Special Services there is an *added* reluctance to acknowledge each other. I have never seen security so tight – and of course it's natural, you must see that. Every group feels that it alone is *chiefly* responsible for the safety of the Person and that if it gives any information at all to the other group that other group may jump the gun and wreck the most carefully made plans. And it is the *Person* whose life is in danger.'

'Do what you can,' I said. It wasn't really meant to rile him. He was doing all he could and I knew it. But I had the set-up on ice now and it was all I could think about. I was scared that something would bust it up – something like a last-minute decision by the Bangkok security people to take the Link Road off the itinerary.

It wouldn't worry Kuo. He had a cell of four picked marksmen and he would just shift the pattern so that whatever route the motorcade used it would come under fire from one of them, with Kuo himself manning the most likely area. There is only a given number of main streets in any city where a public procession can be run: you cannot, in London, send it up and down Curzon Street and Half Moon Street to avoid Piccadilly.

Loman hadn't answered. He had gone off on one of his therapeutic walks around the empty crates to get his anger down. I was sorry for him. I had once seen him briefing five crack operators at the Bureau, giving them a mission as complicated as an electronic computer – access, courier-lines, letter-drops, radio hook-up, cover-stories, timing-factors, liaison patterns and the whole picture, all within one hour because there was a plane waiting and the complete operation depended on moonlight. It was a masterpiece and nothing went wrong.

But he was out here on the far side of the world from his natural base with only an Embassy to work on instead of fifty official departments and reference sources and with one single bloody-minded agent who'd sold him a set-up that had shocked him to the guts.

Next time he'd choose someone else and Amen to that.

'One thing I want to know,' I said when he came up to have another look at me. 'You're trying hard to get information out of the security people at the Embassy. How hard are *they* trying to get information out of you?'

He was suddenly interested. It was just a flicker of the eyes but even in the poor light I caught it.

'Everyone is trying to keep information from the other groups, as I have just said. It's just as natural that everyone is also trying to *get* it.'

'I'm still waiting, Loman.'

He said obliquely: 'It's part of my task as your director to attend to every fringe aspect of the mission and leave you to concentrate on the actual – '

'The one that's trying the hardest is the Maine girl, correct?'

'I really can't expose you to problems that – '

'She's outside now, did you know? She tagged you here, did you know?'

His face went stiff. 'But I took every *possible* – '

'Look, it was bound to happen. The minute you sanctioned my operation I cleared out of the hotel and went to ground and she lost me for the first time in fifteen days and it must have sent her hysterical. You're my only contact and she knows it because I asked for you by name at the Embassy the first time I met her there, so she's had you tagged since she lost me – must have. She needs me badly and all I want to know is why. And all you have to do is tell me.'

He didn't provoke me by asking if I were certain she was there outside. It was my job to know where people were. He hadn't sensed the tag because he wasn't an agent in the field – he was an executive who did most of his work at a desk. But I had checked him for tags every time we had met since I'd left the Pakchong Hotel and tonight he wasn't clean: she'd been using one of the cover-availabilities I'd examined in the alley – the fuel-oil tank on the timber props.

'I am very disturbed to – '

'It doesn't matter,' I said. 'You're not expected to know the drill. That's why I always make sure you're the first to arrive. Just tell me what she wants.'

'I don't know.' He said it quite spontaneously and I knew he wasn't lying. It always has to be watched: a good intelligence director will tell his agent precisely what he chooses, precisely what is good for him, and will lie his way out of any risk that his agent will be worried or confused by anything that he does not specifically need to know. An agent is sent like a ferret into a hole and he is not told if there is a dog at the other end. It's Control that takes care of the dog.

I said: 'You don't know? But you must have some ideas. I'm in a red sector now, Loman. I can't trust in Local Control Bangkok to deal with fringe aspects for me while I'm in the field because Local Control Bangkok is one man: you. And it isn't your field.'

He said nothing, but he compromised: he didn't walk away. I knew he was worried about loss of face because he hadn't sensed the tag but he could worry about it some other time when I didn't need him. I said:

'She's trying to milk us, isn't she? Her group's been following me ever since I took the mission over. I do the work, they get the results. If they want to protect the Person they'll have to do it on their own and in their own way. You know the danger – if they baulk me now it can spoil my aim and we'll miss. You know the risk. Call it a national tragedy.'

He studied my face for a bit and then broke a rule because he had to, because he was Local Control Bangkok and one man wasn't enough to keep an agent alive in a red sector.

'They're not concerned,' he said, 'with protecting the Person.'

'Is that an idea or do you know for certain?'

'I've told you, I don't *know* anything. You asked for my ideas. The Maine group isn't trying to get information about the Person, from me or anyone else. They're not interested in the official arrangements or the itinerary or the Kuo set-up.' To prove his worth as a director and save some of his face he said parsonically: 'That is why I made no comment when you twice asked me about the woman. My conviction was that her group was not running a mission similar to yours and was therefore unlikely to get in your way. That is still my conviction and I still believe it's my duty to tell you simply to forget it and concentrate on your operation.'

But I knew he was ready to talk so I didn't waste time on persuasion. I told him:

'Stick to principles and you'll have a death on your hands. His. And maybe mine. If they're not on a protection mission what's their field?'

'They *are* on a protection mission.'

'But you said – '

'Their mission is not to protect the Person. It's to protect you.'

I shut up because I had to think.

It checked. They had been tagging me – the woman herself and the two men, the thin one and the one with the splay-footed walk – and no one else. They had seen that I was logging the Kuo travel-pattern but they had never switched their attention from me to him, and when I lost him they went on tagging me; they weren't interested in Kuo. And the woman had been there at the airport 'in case I took a plane'.

The kites had begun moving.

We are too old, too animal, to let ourselves become lost in thought, lost to our environments. Our environments are the jungle. A draught from the street had begun moving the kites and they danced grotesquely, the big male *chulas* and the female *pakpaos*. Someone had opened a door, so I spoke more loudly: 'Then tell them to get out of my field.' Loman composed his face in suffering, thinking I had raised my voice merely in anger. 'Go out and pick up Scarface and tell her to mother someone else's chick – I'm a big boy now. The only protection I need is from her. I'm relying on you to do that for me, Loman, strictly urgent.' I took the photograph from him and turned away. 'Ten minutes be enough? Then I'm leaving. Clean.'

It would be no good putting the Rifle Club's thousand-yard range anywhere else, because Bangkok is surrounded by rice.

The heat-shimmer spreading from the rice-fields grows steadily worse as the day advances, and makes for a distortion-factor with telescopic sights. I therefore drove eastwards out of the city early enough to put in a couple of hours on the range while the air was stable.

There had been no time to catch the light after leaving the kite warehouse the previous afternoon. I had gone to ground in the condemned building as soon as the area had been checked for tags. I had seen neither Loman nor the girl outside the warehouse: he must have snatched her or scared her off.

This morning the air was gold and nothing showed in my mirror but I selected a couple of harmless-looking saloons and kept between them to make it difficult for anyone to raid me either with a shot or a smash.

My membership card got me straight through to the butts and for the first hour I was alone with the Husqvarna. The dealer had sent it to the Club for me on my instructions, with the scope-sight already mounted. My needs had been for a big bore rifle capable of long-range accurate fire with a heavy, compact bullet achieving high velocity and killing-power. It was thus necessary to choose a bolt-action, which is the slowest of all repeaters for follow-up shots; but it is the most reliable.

All the Husqvarnas are beautiful but the finest they make is the 561. It is a ·358 Magnum, centre-fire, with a three-shot magazine, 25½-inch barrel, hand-chequered walnut stock, corrugated butt-plate and sling swivels. The fore-end and pistol-grip are tipped with rosewood. The total weight is 7¾lbs and the breech-pressure is in the region of 20 tons p.s.i., giving a high muzzle-velocity and an almost flat trajectory with a 150-grain bullet.

A rifle is no better than its sights, so I had chosen an exemplary Balvar 5 by Bausch and Lomb with an optical variable from × 2½ to × 5. Its feature is that as the magnification power is increased the cross-hair reticle remains constant in size and does not tend to obscure the target.

The report and recoil of a big gun are fairly massive and I went to the range partly to learn the Husqvarna's characteristics and align the high overbore scope-sight and partly to condition my nervous system to the unaccustomed shock effect. The eye must get used to the close-up shrouding of the sight-mounting and the figures on the lens; the ear must learn to ignore the heavy percussion of the report; the shoulder must resist the blow of the recoil; above all the perfect marriage must be made between the index finger and the trigger so that, shot after shot, the automatic memory of the finger-muscles takes over from the fore-brain and provides a confident pull through the double springs that will not deflect the aim.

In two hours I put in fifty or sixty shots, taking time and care, checking the target and resetting the alignment of the scope, gradually allowing the negative feedback data to correct the aim until I was bunching a dozen inside the ten-ring. Then I stopped. The flinch that had accompanied the first shots had been exorcized; the right shoulder throbbed but had got the measure of the recoil; the eye was so used to the reticle that as I walked back to the club-house the after-image was superimposed on my vision, true to Emmert's Law.

True to my own law I was ready for Kuo.

It had been unsafe to ask anyone at the Club to deliver the Husqvarna: there was no one to receive it at the condemned building or the kite warehouse and I had no other reliable port of call. I therefore took it with me in the Toyota as far as the new car park just off Rama IV near the Link Road and walked from there, rounding three blocks to make sure of security.

Bangkok is a city whose temples have towers of gold and there are men of subtle style who must choose gold cloth for the adornment of their ritual.

I made my way to the condemned building like an unsuccessful salesman, a roll of cheap carpet under my arm.

Chapter Eleven

THE SCHEDULE

My last meeting with Loman before the day of the action took place at midnight on the 28th. He was much affected by the news that had gone out on the radio a few hours earlier.

In the sultry heat of the warehouse he looked cold, and as he talked to me his white face floated against the colours of the hanging kites. His eyes were bright but the rest of the polish had gone: it had been rubbed off, over the days, by the gradual realization of what he had set in train when he had first proposed to the Bureau in London that he should personally direct an agent to combat the assassination threat, and that the agent should be myself.

Loman had handled big operations involving the life and death of men who worked for him and the fact that three of his agents had lost their lives under his direction was to his credit: a less brilliant officer would have suffered greater losses in the achievement of similar ends. He had taken risks – personal and physical risks – in the actual field and had proved his ordinary courage, as distinct from the extraordinary courage of responsibility to those men whom he sent out on missions known to be grossly dangerous.

But he had never exposed himself to the risk of failing in a mission that had to be carried through in the glare of international limelight, and that concerned the safety of a man whose death would grievously shock the whole of the civilized world.

The effects of even a big intelligence operation are never dramatic except to those who are immediately involved. The public reads that a Russian–Canadian wheat deal has fallen through, that the US has withdrawn one of her nuclear submarine bases from Spain, that General X has resigned his post as Coordinator to the Combined Services Division. The public is not told that such events are often the outcome of intelligence missions and that the success of a given mission had depended upon the illegal duplicating of a certain document, or a journey by an unknown man across a certain frontier with a microdot apparatus strapped beneath the chassis of his car, or the placing of a bang-destruction unit inside the cupboard where a certain Foreign Office messenger keeps his despatch bag.

It may happen that the unknown man crossing the frontier is arrested, searched and detained, and is subsequently shot dead trying to escape. A bang-destruction unit has twice been known to start a major fire and burn the building down. Small beer: the world goes on with its turning.

The mission inaugurated by Loman was unique. Worse, he was in the field with it. Worse still, he had persuaded the Bureau to let him mount a routine operation that really belonged to other parties and had then been himself persuaded by a wildcat agent to sanction homicide as the mainspring of 'the most sensitive operation he had ever been presented with'.

The polish was gone. The shine was off the plum and the fruit was bitter.

His own fault.

'Have you been tuned in?' he asked me sombrely.

I said I had. Since yesterday my intelligence sources had been implemented by a pocket-size transistor and I had sat with it in the quiet of the condemned building with the volume turned right down and the speaker-grille pressed against my ear. There was an hourly broadcast every day until midnight giving the latest details of the official arrangements, and there were clues to be had. A visit to the Children's Hospital would include Rajvithit Road; a stop at the Lumpini Boxing Stadium would take in part of Rama IV. No plans were 'as yet definite' (the Home Office was still obviously worried), but there were some significant pointers buried among the handouts: the staff of the Children's Hospital were looking 'very spruce in their new uniforms as a result of the Charity Drive'; Butri and Kaewsanan, two of Thailand's champion boxers, had been engaged in 'an entertaining series of training fights' for the past few days.

It was bad security on the part of the authorities and I was grateful. I still had to know the itinerary before we could be certain the set-up would work.

The main item of news had come in at 9.30 p.m. that night. Prince Udom had been taken ill.

'What's your reaction?' Loman asked me.

'Does it make any difference?' Prince Udom was to have

accompanied the Person in the motorcade, sitting at his side in the Cadillac. 'Either he's got cold feet or the Government's put pressure on him to keep out of danger, since he's a Minister and the strong man of the Cabinet.'

'In either case the Palace fears an attempt.'

I looked at him in the dim light. 'You must be pretty far gone. The Palace fears an attempt? We're better informed. I've seen the gun delivered and located the sniping-post and got a picture of the man who's going to do the job. Are you worried because the Palace *fears* what we *know*?'

'I mean,' he said bleakly, 'that it won't make things easier for us if the general alarm sets in. They might decide to change the itinerary.'

'There'd be some point to that if we knew what the itinerary was.'

'We know.'

'Come on, then.'

'It will go via the Link Road.'

'Thank Christ.'

So it was on. The set-up would work. The rendezvous was safe. The temple, the condemned building, Kuo, the Husqvarna – the gold cloth and the cheap carpet and the flowers and the crowd and with luck the overkill. I asked him: 'How did you get it, Loman?'

'From Pangsapa.' He had an odd look in his eyes because of the way I'd spoken – I'd sounded jubilant. Why shouldn't I? It was what I was here for. Kuo. 'He made contact,' Loman said. 'He gave me the whole route.'

'Anything else?'

'One item. He reports that another man has joined the Kuo cell.'

'Total of seven? Let 'em all come.' I should have given it thought. I didn't; I was too busy feeling cocky, kicking my heels. 'What was Pangsapa's price?'

'He didn't ask for payment.'

'Civil of him.'

Pangsapa had a nose for a bargain: it would pay him to keep in with us and share the success. It would cost us nothing but the slight trouble, afterwards, of confirming officially that he had helped to safeguard the guest of his own beloved country. Loman wasn't the only one eager for honours, but Pangsapa would use them to gain favour in high places. Inspection of his shipments would become perfunctory.

'He urged me to keep him in contact with us,' Loman said, 'so that he can signal further information as soon as he has any.'

'All right,' I said, 'but don't lead him to me – don't let him know where I am. Look out for tags – he hung one on me when I left his office two days ago and I had to flush him. Don't let him crash the party. What about Scarface – did you warn her off me?'

'She wasn't outside when I looked for her – '

'You bet she wasn't.'

'I found she was tagging me, as soon as – '

'You bet she was. Hoping you'd lead her back to me at some new place where we thought we'd be safe.'

'I just led her to the Embassy.' He added reflectively, 'She's with Mil. 6, you know.'

'She's *what*?'

'Someone tipped me off.'

'Mil. 6 is protecting the *Bureau*? From what? From precisely what?'

He said tonelessly: 'We don't know. That's just it. We don't know.'

'Jesus Christ – the blind leading the blind!' But something warned me. I was too jubilant, too cocky. Everything was set up: the rendezvous, Kuo, the Husqvarna – but there was this thing, this damned thing, that didn't fit into any pattern at all. I don't like mysteries.

The bounce had gone out of me. Like poor old Loman I was sobering up. 'From Kuo?' I asked him.

'What?'

'Does Mil. 6 think it can protect me from the Kuo cell?'

'You are in no danger from Kuo. He is in danger from you.'

'All right, what are they trying to protect me from?'

The coloured kites hung motionless, muffling any echo, but it seemed my question echoed and I wished I could have bitten it back. I was getting too interested in my own skin, getting frightened because there was something I didn't know about, couldn't recognize, couldn't fit in with known patterns. Stomach-think. Unhealthy. Let fear take over and you're in the worst danger of all: danger from yourself.

There was only Kuo I had to deal with and he was a sitting duck.

Whatever it was that I didn't know about wasn't important. It seemed important just because I didn't know about it. Turn the bloody thing inside out, make it make sense. Rationalize, brain-think it out and forget it.

There are always areas of the unknown in any operation. You start your mission and you light your lamps as you go, picking your way through the dark, making your journey from lamp to lamp and never looking back. But there are patches of dark and you skirt them, have to, because your lamps are too small to show you everything. They light only the way.

The kites hung without moving, their shapes strange and their colours garish and meaningless. Those nearest me were well defined, identifiable. The others, gathered behind them in the deeper gloom, were the hosts of the unknown.

I must needs take comfort in the ancient law of my trade. Fear springs from imagination and without imagination we cannot survive.

Loman hadn't answered me. It didn't matter. The question shouldn't have been asked. I said:

'Let's have the dope. Schedule, people, so forth.'

'Very well.' He looked more confident. This was his home ground. 'The schedule remains unchanged. The Person will arrive Bangkok tomorrow at 11.50 hours in an aircraft of the Queen's Flight captained by J. F. Wooldridge. On board will be Wing Commander G. M. G. Thompson, medical officer, Rear Admiral Charles Nixon-Thorpe, Superintendent Forsythe and Inspector L. W. Johns, Special Branch.'

Larry Johns. They'd blown up a River Police launch from under us on the Estuary thing in 1961. What was he doing shepherding VIPs?

'The plane will be met by HRH Prince Ruchirawong, Foreign Minister, Marshal Sumate Photicharoen, Governor of Bangkok, General Luen Punnaken of the Army, Air Marshal Gorinajdeja, Admiral Suwannasorn, Sir William Cole-Verity, British Ambassador. Others present – '

'Will you be there?'

'Of course.'

'Is that when you start calling me up?'

He had sold me the idea of a two-way radio to keep me in touch with what went on. Since radios can become jammed inadvertently I had insisted on a fail-safe in Lumpini Park: a boy with a kite.

He said: 'They leave the airport at 12.05, arriving at the Palace at 13.00. That is when you'll receive my introductory signal. Leaving the Palace after luncheon the Person arrives at the Embassy at 15.25. He will stop there for fifteen minutes to congratulate the Ambassador's staff on the success of British Week. He will therefore leave the Embassy at 15.40 and take the shortest route to Rama IV by Lumpini Park, turning right towards the Link Road.'

'No stops?'

'No.' He drew a breath and got it over quickly: 'The motorcade will arrive at the Link Road at 15.50 or thereabouts.'

Ten minutes to four. The rendezvous. There'd be a bit of heat-haze but less exhaust-gas than there was normally because traffic would have been stopped. It wasn't a bad time of day for the job.

I looked at my watch.

'Fair enough. Fifteen hours from now. Then you're off the hook.'

'The mission will be over,' he replied thinly, 'whichever way it goes.'

'I'll tell you which way it'll go. You haven't pushed me up and down every bloody street in this town for nothing. One fine day you'll get your gong, Loman.'

He didn't answer. His anxiety even inhibited anger. I asked him: 'Only one thing left. What reactions have they been getting from the Person?'

'They've had a lot of trouble with him, of course. He's very difficult to handle in a case like this. He has refused to let them put *any* of the shields on the car.'

'Rear plastic quarter-light?'

'Including that.'

It was important. The rear shield would cover a following shot if for any reason at all Kuo failed to make a kill head-on. The oriels formed a ring round the temple and there was a gallery inside, and he could move round within 180° if he had to. No shield: no cover. I said:

'Then I won't have to miss.'

He looked away. The subject was distasteful to him.

Then he shouldn't mix with the wrong people.

I said: 'Why didn't the Palace override his orders?'

'They tried. The King had given instructions about shields but the Person got wind of it and wrote him a private letter. The gist of it was a reminder that his Majesty had been pleased to drive through the city of London in an open car at the time of his State Visit. It was suggested that the rigors of an English April were surely more treacherous to the health than any inclemency to be offered by the fair city of Bangkok.'

'Public Relations stuff?'

'No. The letter was vouched for. You know how private a letter is, once the tenth secretary has passed it on for filing. Besides, it's typical. Public Relations have put out their version to the *Evening Standard*: "I want to be able to see the people, and some of them may want to see me." Behind the whole story is of course a very definite injunction: no shields. And behind the decision is his personal view of the whole situation: he feels he will best serve his country by demonstrating that anonymous threats are for the waste-paper basket.' He looked down at his feet again, away from my eyes. 'I rather wish we weren't so responsible for the safety of quite so good a man.'

'I've told you,' I said, 'I'd do it for the postman.'

His bright eyes came at me again – 'But it's a matter of consequences, isn't it? You must have given it *some* thought.'

'All right, you tell me. You've got one foot in the Embassy and the other in London. What are the consequences if we miss? Another Sarajevo?'

'I don't know.' Almost petulantly he said: 'I've never worked in an area of which I've known so little.'

'We'll know a bit more tomorrow.'

His mouth quivered silently, blocked by a rush of too many words. He was really very cross with me. He finally managed to speak. 'I wish I had your limited view, Quiller.'

'My view's limited by crossed hairs in a circle. Someone's got to concentrate on that. You look after the consequences while I pop the weasel. Then there won't be any.'

'How much,' he asked me as if I'd never spoken, 'do you think Kuo will be paid? If he succeeds?'

'He doesn't work that way. The cost of a dead body is a few bob and the cost of a bullet is a few pence. It's the set-up that's expensive and the fee's already in his pocket. I'd put it at five hundred thousand pounds.'

Loman nodded. 'Who can afford a sum like that? Only a government. That's why I cannot ignore the question of consequences.'

I turned away from him. He could stay awake all night if he wanted to. I had to be fresh for the job.

'Worry it,' I said, turning again and watching him from a little distance. 'Worry it out. I've got my limited view. All I need to know is that the consequences of crooking the index finger are a hole in a skull.'

He didn't answer. I shall always remember him standing there among the coloured kites, fearful and bright of eye, wondering what he'd got into and wondering how to get out. It was easier for me and my terms were simpler. A dog hungered for dog.

'Good night, Loman.'

It was the last time I saw him before the kill.

Chapter Twelve

THE SET-UP

One of the vital duties of an intelligence officer is to see that the agent he is directing in the field is left unworried by every aspect of the mission that does not directly concern him.

Thus Loman had angered me because he had broken his rule and tried to saddle me with considerations of the *consequences*. But I knew that subconsciously he was rationalizing and that the real basis of his fear was more personal, more intimate and more closely concerned with my precise operation than any general thoughts on wide-scale repercussions. He was worried because:

I had to kill.

I might fail to kill.

I might kill for nothing.

And whichever way it went he was going to lose: because one of those things was going to happen.

That was why he had immediately refused to sanction my proposed operation when I put it to him in our room in Soi Suek 3 and why I had to work on him so hard to make him finally agree. He knew at the outset that one of those three things was going to happen and his real struggle had been to decide whether it was worth it.

I don't think he ever reached a conclusion. He reached a decision – to sanction my proposal – but he was never certain how much it would be worth letting me do what I wanted. He brought me to the day of the 29th in the hope – and nothing more than the hope – that we would be proved right in allowing the mission to swerve into this new and very dangerous direction.

That was why he had talked about consequences, the last time I saw him before the action. But I think he meant the consequences to us, not to the broad South-East Asian scene.

My proposal could not have been more simple. It comprised seven factors with two corollaries.

(1) Although there was a threat to assassinate a British subject the responsibility for his protection rested with the Thai Government.

(2) Those few British groups who were able to set up collateral protection (whether officially recognized in that role by the Thai Government or not) were the Special Branch protection officers, Security, MI 6 and fringe departments at the British Embassy, Bangkok. And they would work on their own according to the long-established tradition of inter-Services rivalry.

(3) Loman and I could not – even through our Bureau in London – convince either the Thai Security forces (Colonel Ramin) or the British groups of the danger to be expected from Kuo, because it would imply lack of efficiency on their part. Further, we did not exist; therefore it would be similar to an unknown herbalist seeking to advise a panel of Harley Street surgeons.

(4) For the same reason – that the Bureau does not exist – we could do nothing officially. We could not warn, advise or call upon anyone at all, anywhere.

(5) Supposing for a moment that we could warn Colonel Ramin of the danger expected from Kuo, he might feel disposed to hunt him and arrest him on suspicion. But from my intimate knowledge of Kuo, gained during many days of observation and conclusions, it would then be left to one or more of his cell to proceed with their plans for the assassination – and Colonel Ramin would not even concern himself, since the chief danger would seem to have been eliminated by Kuo's arrest.

(6) Therefore, we had no hope of invoking Colonel Ramin's co-operation to any useful effect. It was pointless to insist that he took action against Kuo because if he took action the danger would remain.

(7) It was to be hoped that the Thai Home Office departments – Security, CID and Metropolitan Police – plus the small British groups offering collateral protection, would succeed in stopping an assassination attempt. But if they failed we would try to prevent it by a last ditch action.

The two corollaries were:

(1) Loman's ability to sanction homicide was by virtue of the fact that the Bureau does not exist. Discipline within its own walls is uncompromising, but it is not officially responsible to any department or minister. It can operate only on the understanding that it fills a gap in the intelligence complex, that it takes no action without the most serious pre-thinking, and that if an

action falls outside the dictates of national and international law it will guarantee to take its own can back in the event of exposure and will involve no one else. There are many reasons why the existence of the Bureau is officially denied but the most important reason is that it sometimes resorts to illegal methods for the sake of expediency. These include homicide.

(2) Given that Loman, as my intelligence director, was able to consider sanctioning an act of homicide, it could not take the form of random murder. On the principle that we suspected Kuo to have arrived in Bangkok for the purpose of assassination I could have killed him out of hand before now. Up to the time of his going to ground there had been many opportunities. But Loman had rightly made the proviso that if we were to kill a man we must kill him in the very act of attempting the thing we had to prevent. Otherwise we would never be sure of our moral right to do it. There was only one time, then, and one place where he should be killed: at what I had now come to think of as the 'rendezvous' – a word expressing both a time and place. (There was another reason why we could not kill Kuo at any time prior to the 29th. It would have been as useless as Colonel Ramin's arresting him: the danger from the Kuo *cell* would remain. For the record, this was not our chief reason for holding fire. The Bureau follows the tenets of jungle justice.)

Summarizing: my proposal to Loman was that if all else failed and it was up to us to stop an assassination, we must let Kuo plan his set-up and perfect it, so that once his finger was on the trigger *there would be no time for him to put a reserve plan into operation.* It was feasible that he would post a guard inside the doorway of the temple, so that even if Colonel Ramin decided to search the place and arrest Kuo at the fifty-ninth minute as the motorcade entered the Link Road, the guard could make a prearranged signal to a reserve marksman in the area who was briefed to shoot in those circumstances. That would be a professional set-up, and Kuo was a professional.

Regardless of whatever action both the Thai and British protection groups would take there was only one method that was a hundred per cent certain: to shoot first, and at the last minute. In three major waves of arrests the police had neutralized upwards of two hundred known agitators, subversive elements and Communist agents as part of their 'drive against crime'. Today, on the morning of the 29th, a thousand police were combing five thousand unoccupied rooms along the motorcade route. Uncountable bouquets of flowers would be examined for hidden bombs. But the only certainty lay in an overkill.

Loman was worried because in sanctioning my proposal he was going to let one of three things happen. If I killed Kuo it would be premeditated, and if I were caught and put on trial I would have to involve others in my defence, however indirectly, in order to plead justifiable homicide; and the Bureau would be seen suddenly to exist; and in the moment of its existence it would be blown apart. If I failed to kill, because of the heat-haze or sweat on my finger or a fault in the mechanism of the gun, the Person would suffer public execution. If I killed for nothing – that is, if Kuo had arranged for a reserve marksman to take over – *whatever happened to Kuo himself*, the Person would still be shot dead.

Loman had angered me by voicing his fears, even though they were not his true fears. He had angered me not by breaking a rule strictly enforced on intelligence directors in the Bureau but by reminding me of my own fears, the ones that were with me now as I crouched in the small high room of the condemned building, the Husqvarna across my knees.

Let him be damned for that.

For me the day passed slowly through three stages.

During the first few hours of the morning the Link Road below my window looked fairly normal, the only difference being that it was a national holiday and the pavements were filled with strollers.

At eleven o'clock I heard the news on my transistor. The main item was that Prince Udom had passed a comfortable night but was expected to be confined to his bed for several days. His place beside the distinguished visitor was to be taken by HRH Prince Rajadhon, who was on leave from his studies at Basle University in order to participate in the Palace receptions.

The news contained an announcement of the definite itinerary of the motorcade. (Pangsapa's information to Loman was perfectly correct.) It was the first time the exact route had been made public, and within half an hour the strollers on the pavement below the condemned building had grown thicker, and the police began setting up guard-ropes on each side of the road. Motor-cycle patrols were now slowing the traffic because of danger to the crowds.

Halfway between the condemned building and the temple the Link Road curved at a boomerang angle of some 150° and the people pressed more thickly at that point because it offered a better view.

The street looked pretty: flags, flowers, bunting, women in silk. Soon after two o'clock the traffic was diverted along Rama IV and the Link Road was quiet except for the voices of the crowd. A chapter of Brahman priests made a patch of bright yellow among the other colours. The sun was hot and parasols opened like big flowers; soft-drinks men worked their way through. Small children were delighted as their fathers lifted them to let them look. The police moved systematically, taking the bouquets from some of the women and weighing them briefly, handing them back.

First-aid men of the Thai Red Cross had posted themselves at intervals along the guard-ropes.

I heard a door open below me in the building. I had been listening for it and went along to the elevator. The voices of the policemen were amplified by the central well of the staircase and other doors banged as they began searching the second floor. I went into the elevator. There was no electric power in the place; it had been cut off when the building was marked down for demolition; but I had tested the manual emergency handle the day before and now I turned it, winding the elevator down to the blank walls between the fifth and sixth floors. All my gear was with me, leaving the room bare for the inspection. Cheap carpet, sleeping-bag, tripod and camera, field-glasses and gun. It looked like a second-hand store.

I waited. Their footsteps echoed sharply on the stairs. They opened every door, calling to one another. Colonel Ramin was being very thorough. The blanket-operation of a whole-scale search is typical police routine and in most cases it is of value. Even on this day it had a certain advantage: the Colonel would be able to claim, later, that his men had searched every room.

They reached the top floor. I stood watching one of the elevator cables which was frayed: two strands had parted, the ends curling; in the bottom of each curl was a crescent of dust and plaster congealed by the damp that had leaked through the roof. The cable would never be repaired now.

They were taking their time. The heat was stifling but it was a stray thought that made the sweat spring: would the emergency handle still work all right when they had gone? How much would the South-East Asian complex of war-brink policies be affected by one man getting stuck in an elevator?

My watch said 3.15 p.m. and Loman would be calling again in ten minutes if the schedule were running to time. I checked the setting of the two-way radio again to make sure Loman couldn't signal. That was bad: you shouldn't have to check things more than once, at a time when the nerves ought to be at their optimum pitch about two-thirds up the scale.

In the heat I could smell the oil on the mechanism of the gun. A sound came and one of them opened the metal doors above me on the sixth floor to see if anyone were on the roof of the elevator. No one was so he shut the gates. Thoroughness is an admirable quality. I had been thorough too: there was a main emergency handle in the elevator-well at ground level for winding it up and down, and yesterday I had taken the grub-screw out.

The first of them began going back to the stairs and when the rest followed I looked at my watch again. It was running it close for Loman's next call. The main exit doors were slamming shut and I waited another minute and then grasped the handle, overcame the half-second of irrational fear that it wouldn't work, and wound the elevator back to the top floor.

A lot of the stuff could stay where it was; all I needed was the carpet, the tripod and the gun. The Jupiters gave × 8 magnification and the Balvar scope only × 5, but since first light this morning I had stopped using the field-glasses so that I could get used to the scope. It was the scope that would give me my last sight of him.

The second stage of the day began now. The police had made their search and the main doors below had been shut. Yesterday I had made a hole in the plaster above the door of my room with a rusty nail and now I hung up the cheap carpet. This was sufficient. The sound of the report would be trapped before it reached the ground floor inside the building; the main doors would provide additional silencing. Most of the sound would remain trapped in the room itself because the Husqvarna would be mounted far back from the window. The residual sound would be diffused in the open air, impossible to place because of the height of the window from the street.

The second stage of the day was easier than the first. There had been a lot of last-minute doubts to cope with mentally and they had been worrying until I caught the first sign of movement in the middle oriel of the Phra Chula Chedi. With the Husqvarna resting on the camera tripod I took three sightings within half an hour. The details of his face were blurred by the heat-haze but every time he stopped moving I found I could keep the point of the cross-hairs within the target area: the face and head. When the time came he would be perfectly still, in the same attitude as I.

The most worrying doubt was now eliminated: the rendezvous would be kept.

Loman had called me up for the first time at one o'clock. From that moment the whole mission suddenly became real for me and I understood the measure of the thing he had taken on. Last night in the kite warehouse I hadn't grasped it. All he said on the radio was:

'*He has arrived at the Palace.*'

Until that moment the Bureau's 9th Directive hadn't been much more than a theoretical exercise, a practice operation, interesting but without substance. The Person was very much a part of his official background, a public figure pursuing his onerous affairs for the public good, essentially a Londoner, his image inseparable from the image of tall gates and monuments, Westminster and the Mall. London was a far cry from this city of golden towers where the petals of magnolia fell to the monsoon wind, but suddenly he was here among us and the theory and practice took on substance and the mission was thrust into our hands, cold, hard and uncompromising as a cocked gun.

Chapter Thirteen

OVERKILL

Isolated in the small high room of the condemned building I was kept in touch with events by the transistor and two-way radio. A general report was now in from Loman and it added a few details to the public announcements. It was as follows:

The arrival of the Person at Don Muang Airport was without incident. He looked very fit and said he was delighted to see the sunshine. There was great enthusiasm from a large crowd The police were present in strength. It was confirmed that Forsythe and Johns of the Special Branch were accompanying the Person. Prince Rajadhon was among the official welcoming party and it was therefore certain that he would take his place beside his distinguished guest in the public procession. Details of this had now been made official: the motorcade would be led by ten motor-cycle outriders of the Bangkok Metropolitan Police. Travelling in the royal car would be the Person, Prince Rajadhon, the British Ambassador, the First Counsellor of the British Embassy and two bodyguards of the King's Household. The second and third cars would contain ministers, equerries and security men. The central section of the motorcade would be flanked by twelve outriders and there would be a rearguard of fifteen motor-cycle police. All officers would be armed.

Some time before my building was entered and searched there had been a further signal from Loman and for the first time there was the suggestion of nerves in his voice.

'The motorcade has just left the Palace and is now heading north towards Rajdamnoen Central Avenue.'

It was from that point that the worst of the waiting began. It was broken up by the police-search of the building but once I had gone back to my room and fixed the carpet over the door there was nothing else to do.

Loman was buzzing for me so I switched the radio to 'receive'.

'Can you hear me, Quiller?'

'Go ahead,' I said. There'd been fright in his tone. He must have thought the radio had packed up.

'*Is everything in order?*' Still talked like a bloody textbook.

'Yes. Police have made their search. On my own now and all set.'

There was silence and then he came in again, his tone a bit steadier.

'*Five-minute halt at Government House. Next half will be at the Embassy.*'

I acknowledged and switched to 'stand-by'.

The sound of the crowd floated up on the warm air; it was like a vast aviary, the women's voices pitched sharply, the children piping now and then in little bird-cries. It was odd not to hear the traffic. I kept away from the window now.

When I took a sighting through the Balvar scope it picked up movement at once in the oriel of the temple. He still had the smoked glasses on; I had never seen him without them. I wondered how he was feeling. He was a professional and he'd done this before but he was putting something like half a million on one shot and that would be important to him. There would be time to get in a second and even a third, even with a bolt-action, but it was the first that would count because it would be unhurried, a slow sure pull against the springs. A second or third shot would be affected by the knowledge of a miss, a nervous block difficult to get through because the aim had to be *better*, not just *as good*.

He wouldn't miss. He was Kuo the Mongolian.

There would be a period of some ten seconds in which he – and I – must operate.

The signal sounded and I switched to 'receive'.

'*Can you hear me, Quiller?*'

'Go ahead.'

'*The motorcade has arrived at the Embassy. They will be here for fifteen minutes. After ten minutes from now – at 15.35 – I want you to keep open for me. Please acknowledge.*'

'Keep open from 15.35. Will do.'

I cut him out. I didn't like the sound of his voice. It wasn't just speaker-distortion; there was a scream of fright trying to push out past every word.

A period, yes, of some ten seconds in which Kuo and I must operate. It would begin when he sighted the vanguard of police outriders coming into the Link Road and it would end when the leading car of the motorcade was lost from his sight below the trees of the temple gardens. Putting it more precisely the period of time was – for me alone – narrowed down to about half, because I would wait until he raised his gun. I had decided on that without reference to Loman, without reference to anything really. It seemed good manners. *M'sieur, tirez le premier.* Or try.

The noise of the crowd was making me restive; I wanted to look down from the window, to look at the road where it curved through the gay colours of the silks and the flowers and the parasols. I mustn't go near the window.

The room was very hot and I had to keep wiping my hands. From the back of the room all I could see was the great gold dome of the Phra Chula Chedi brilliant against the afternoon sky. And the ring of oriels.

At 1535 I went on to listening watch and after a few minutes Loman came straight through:

'*Can you hear me?*'

'Go ahead.'

He had to talk slowly. It didn't fool me. A dog has a nose for the smell of fear.

'*He is just getting into the car. Prince Rajadhon following.*'

I could hear the crowd in the background.

'*Now the Ambassador.*'

Two muffled reports: the car-doors shutting.

'*The Motorcade is moving off.*'

It was 3.41 p.m.

I said: 'All right, Loman, it's over to me now.'

He began saying something but I cut the switch.

Eight or nine minutes to go. Speed would be 25 m.p.h. or thereabouts. Plern Chit Road, turning right down Vithayu and past the Arabian Embassy, crowds lining the route all the way, Spanish Embassy, flags, flowers, people clapping, Japanese Embassy, children being lifted so that they could see the distinguished man who had come such a long way to visit them. Netherlands Embassy, first-aid parties pressing a gangway for a fainting-case, American Embassy, the soft-drinks men profiting from the heat, the thirst, the excitement .Lumpini Park.

I had already moved to the side of the room and could see the trees of the Park and above them the fragile shape of the kite, yellow with a blue cross, unsteady because there was only a low breeze across the open space of the lawns but lifting higher all the time in little jerks.

The heat seemed worse and the handkerchief was damp from wiping my hands. Three minutes, at the most four. I could see part of the Link Road below the building. Patches of colour, parasols. An ambulance moving very slowly in reverse down the side road, stopping when it reached the back of the crowd. A man selling balloons.

A false alarm – there always is: the roof of a police-car mistaken for the vanguard of the motorcade. The voice of the crowd rising in a sudden wave, subsiding.

About a minute.

The mission had seemed very long, all those weeks, living in the Toyota, living with the Jupiters, learning him like a brother. Soon we would be strangers.

Sound came from the distance, clapping, cheering, at first faint, loudening, so I moved round to the back of the room and wiped the sweat from my hands for the last time, wrists, palms, between the fingers, carefully between the fingers of the right hand.

There was a flat square top to the tripod with a set-screw proud in the centre to take the camera and I had put a cloth pad over it with elastic bands. The blue steel barrel of the Husqvarna had left its impression on the pad from previous sightings. I raised the Husqvarna and laid the barrel across the pad and flicked the safety-catch off. The smell of the machine-oil was strong, a good smell, clean and efficient.

The sound of the crowd was rising in a slow wave from the distance and the people directly below the condemned building began calling his name and I had the cross-hairs centred dead on the face in the oriel.

His gun came up and I saw the long glint of the barrel and my finger took up the tension of the preliminary spring and went on squeezing and when the big Husqvarna kicked I kept the sights on the target and saw redness colour the face and head, but something was wrong because the crowd had begun screaming and I knew that I'd killed for nothing because something was wrong down there.

Chapter Fourteen

SHOCK

Burnt cordite reeked in the room and my head still rang from the explosion.

When I looked down from the window they were still screaming and the change in their sound was terrible: seconds ago they had been calling his name and now they cried out in agony.

It was impossible to focus on details but the overall scene had the dreadful clarity of a slow-motion picture: the vanguard escort had rounded the 150° curve in the road but the royal car had run straight on to plunge into the crowd, and the wall of living bodies had been breached before its momentum was arrested.

The long white Cadillac was halted now in the midst of the swaying people. The vanguard escort was wheeling and coming back. The motor-cycle police on the left flank of the procession were sliding to a stop; the first of these, surprised by the course of the royal car, had swung their machines flat on to their sides in an attempt to avoid ramming the crowd. Petrol had spilled and a spark from the friction of metal against flint had fired a tank and the rider was rolling on the ground to put out the flames that had caught his uniform.

The right flank of the escort was halting and turning back, two of the patrols colliding. The second and third convertibles had slewed to a stop and the rearguard was pulling up.

Stretcher-bearers had already driven a lane through the stricken crowd from the ambulance near the curve and the ambulance itself was backing in their wake with both doors held wide open.

An intermittent buzz began on the floor beside me and I ignored it. Loman was trying to call me up but there was nothing to tell him, nothing that would make sense.

The police were attacking the petrol fire, dragging the overturned machines clear before another tank could catch. Other riders were pressing their way along the front of the crowd and trying to force them back from the flame area – but the crowd was helpless, cut off from escape by its own mass. The ministers and equerries were getting out of the convertibles to help the police.

Sirens began sounding from the distance beyond the temple as the nearest fire-fighting unit was called into action.

The sun made everything bright and the colours of the crowd were gay – flags, flowers, women in silk, the flutter of parasols. The screams still came.

Even from the top floor of the condemned building I could not see what was happening around the royal car because it lay buried in frenzied movement.

It seemed a long way to the elevator, a long time tearing the carpet down from the door and wrenching at the handle, the empty passage, the metal gates. I came back running, knocking the glasses by accident against the door and lunging for the window, kneeling there to focus them and swing the white Cadillac into the centre of the lens.

Loman kept on signalling.

They had put out the flames. Fire-foam smothered people and frothed across the roadway. The chapter of Brahman priests had made their way across and were helping the police. Only two men were still inside the royal car, the driver in the front sitting motionless, another man slumped on the floor at the back. Even through the × 8 Jupiters I could not distinguish the white dress tunic of Prince Rajadhon because the uniforms of the police were also white and the first of them had now reached the royal car.

The crowd was spilling through the broken guard-ropes and the roadway was inundated except for some lanes they were trying to keep open for the evacuation of the injured. Two ambulances of the Thai Red Cross were thrusting their way to the central area.

The screams had died away. There was no more fire.

I picked the radio up and flicked the switch:

'Loman?'

He asked: 'What were those sirens?'

He had been listening to them in the distance, trying to get through to me.

I told him: 'The car left the road and hit the crowd.'

He said something I couldn't catch – just 'God' or something like that. I went on talking. 'A petrol fire started but it's been dealt with. A lot of injured and some dead – it went straight into them. There was an ambulance near the spot and it's just leaving. I can't see much detail.'

When I cut him in he asked: 'What happened to Kuo?'

'He's dead.'

The smell of the cordite was still on the air.

Loman was silent. There was a question he had to ask and it wanted courage. It is always agreeable to make your report at the end of a successful mission. The risks have been taken and the dangers are past and nothing can go wrong any more and you are still by luck alive. In the sight of your director and the whole Bureau you have scored a point; in the sight of whatever paltry gods you call your own you have smashed a hand in the amorphous face of the enemy (whose name is the fear of failure) and earned a perch in whatever far heaven you can fleetingly believe in till it all begins again and your hand – still bruised and bleeding – must smash again into the same face and the same fear and show that the day . . . for another day . . . is yours. Yea, even in your own sight, the one that counts the most.

No go.

'From where you are,' Loman put his question, 'can you see the Person?'

'No.'

Another short silence. 'I'll go down to the Link Road. Contact later.'

When I cut the switch I knew that the mission was over and that it had failed.

So the dog had eaten dog and to no purpose. It crouched, licking its wounds.

I could have stayed in the small high room for a long time, trying to think, to piece together the smashed bits of a mission *manqué* and set the record straight. No one would have found me until they came to knock the building down. But there were some bits missing and I had to go and pick for them among the rubble.

I put everything into the elevator with the rest – the fieldglasses, cheap carpet, tripod, gun, the tools of my trade. And went down by the stairs.

It is difficult to walk without thinking; the body's movement stirs the mind. A few thoughts came: there had been no *accident*,

95

But why had they taken so much trouble, made it so elaborate? Perhaps to be certain. Only in the midst of a dense crowd made powerless by shock could they be absolutely *certain* of getting to him at close hand and killing him before his protectors could reach him. Eight bodyguards and thirty-seven armed police, cut off from him by the living and the injured and the dying and the dead, by one massive psychological barrier: *shock*. Hadn't they been, then, certain of Kuo, of one straight shot from a master-killer?

So many questions. Kuo would answer them.

It wasn't far to the Phra Chula Chedi, the temple with the golden dome. The crowd was greater now because the Link Road was filling from both ends; of the two masks, humour has less appeal for the human heart than tragedy.

I picked and pressed my way; broken parasols and a crushed bouquet; a child crying, a lost shoe; a priest praying, a torn paper flag. Vehicles moved through the narrow lane that had been the road; the sirens had begun again and bells rang for gangway. A crowd is a fever and will not abate until its course is run.

Magnolia blossoms hung across the gates of the temple and the leaves gave shade. The tall doors were open and there was no one inside. The steps began near the great golden Buddha and followed the curving wall, and I climbed them through the cool shadows, reaching the platform that spanned the base of the dome. A spiral staircase twisted upwards from the centre and I climbed again. Sunlight lay in gold bars across the dark trellis ironwork of the stairs; the murmur of the crowd was loudening as I neared the ring of oriels.

At every tenth stair I stopped and listened for any sound from inside the temple because they might come for him soon, not knowing he was dead and unable to join them.

The sunlight struck in from the oriels and for a moment blinded me. I had reached that part of the gallery that faced Lumpini Park, and had to move round past five oriels before coming to the one that was directly opposite the condemned building.

Then I looked at the floor.

In compliance with the rules of international warfare the military bullet is manufactured with a full metal shield so that the lead tip is not exposed and so that no expansion occurs on striking the target. The idea is that unnecessary pain should be avoided. But I had used a game bullet, a high-velocity load with a blunt nose. This type kills quickly by expanding on impact; it provides greater shocking-power and will drop an animal at once if accurately placed. The disadvantage of a heavy-calibre expanding bullet is that it will spoil the meat (in the case of a boar) or spoil the hide (in the case of a tiger).

I had used a 150-grain bullet to ensure a quick kill and this had been achieved, but the effects of the expansion had left the face unrecognizable.

At the last minute before raising his gun he had taken off the smoked glasses: they were folded neatly on the ledge of the oriel. The sunshine fell across the light grey alpaca jacket and the polished shoes; it was only the face that was out of character with so fastidious a man. Perhaps this was his true face, bestial and bloodied, the face of a jungle soul no longer disguisable by the tricks and artifice of civilized dress. Let it be said: a soul not unlike my own; it was only that our laws were different.

Stepping over him to look at the gun I noticed that the gold cuff-links were missing. The sleeves had ordinary buttons. Something was becoming clear to me even before I took up the gun and examined it, and the need to think and think straight was suddenly urgent.

The gun was a cheap thing, a six-shot Yungchow carbine with a redwood butt.

There was no time now to listen for any sound that might come from inside the temple and I bruised a shoulder on the top rail of the spiral staircase as I swung into it and dropped with my feet touching every third step and my hand hitting at the rail. The beams of sunlight flashed across my eyes and the framework shivered under me until I reached the platform and ran for the curving steps that followed the wall below the dome.

The temple was still deserted but three priests in yellow robes stood at the gates in the shade of the magnolias and one of them stepped towards me thinking perhaps I was a thief disturbed, but I ducked clear and reached the road still at a run and made for the bar on the other side, seeing the telephone before there was need to ask for it.

All three lines were busy and I began redialling the numbers without a stop so that the moment a call ended I'd get my chance but it took a dozen go's and I had to stand there thinking about the mission, reviewing the *whole* thing, getting it into perpective – *his* mission, not mine, *Kuo*'s mission, the one I'd never guessed at, the one that he'd so beautifully brought off.

You light your lamps as you go . . . picking your way through the dark . . . There are patches of dark and you skirt them, have to, because your lamps are too small to show you everything . . . everything.

A line cleared at the Embassy.

'Room 6,' I told them, 'give me Room 6.'

Chapter Fifteen

THE SNATCH

I didn't want to talk to Loman yet because he would have a lot of questions to ask and I wanted to be sure I knew the answers.

When I had given the signal to Room 6 I left the bar and walked along the Link Road. The crowd had broken up but the roadway was still full of people talking about the accident. The scene in the centre was different now: the police had made a barrier and there was a water-cart at work where the royal car had come to a stop. The last ambulance had gone. Steam rose as the sun began drying the water that streamed from the pavement on to the road.

The sense of shock still hung over the people and I passed women in tears, their husbands comforting them. Those near the scene of the accident would not easily forget. Reporters were interviewing people and photographers hurried about.

There was no one anywhere near the condemned building because the crowd was still attracting people to the scene at the curve of the Link Road, and I climbed to the top floor in the clammy heat.

Looking down from the window of my room I composed the whole picture in terms of geometry.

Kuo's mission had been to place the shot. Loman and I had known that. The shot was the pivot of the entire operation. But after the shot had been placed the course of the mission had changed completely, and this we had not known. Kuo was a professional and his intelligence was far beyond that required for the efficient handling of a rifle. As precisely and as carefully as a rifle is pieced together from its components he had dovetailed every part of his mission with my own, assembling a set-up in which I took my place as obediently as if I were under his direct orders.

His mission was a total success and all I had to show for weeks of work was the dead man in the Phra Chula Chedi, the seventh man that Pangsapa had told us about, a man who was not Kuo because he wore no cuff-links and because his cheap Yungchow carbine was a weapon that a marksman of Kuo's calibre would never demean himself to use. All I had done was to kill a decoy while Kuo placed his shot.

Rage against one's own stupidity does no good but in the heat of the room I stood shivering.

There was a drawing-pin stuck in the door of the kite warehouse so when I had dumped the useless tools of my trade I phoned Varaphan in Soi Suek 3.

'Is the bloodstone ready for me?'

'There has been so little time. Everyone is always in such a hurry. But you could make enquiries at our workshop if you are passing that way.'

I decided to walk instead of taking a trishaw because the rage was still burning and I had to deal with it before I met Loman. Cold thought was the only antidote.

There were five press-vans parked outside the Embassy and I had to show my pass so that the police could get me through the pack of reporters. They flashed off pictures of me in case I was important. Caption: 'The Man Who Knew Too Little.'

I got shunted into the Cultural Attaché's office again and the girl came in. I hardly recognized her. Everything was the same, beautiful walk, good clothes, an oddness to the left side of the face – but her eyes flickered with the aftermath of shock and her voice had lost its certainty. For the first time she looked like a woman instead of a mechanical goddess.

Maybe I had changed too: she took a few seconds to focus. We stood listening to distant sounds, phonebells and doors, the sounds of a complacent Embassy shaken to the core.

I said: 'Room 6.'

'Yes.' She still didn't move or look away. All the words she wanted to speak, all the questions she wanted to ask were held silent in the flickering of her eyes.

'Did you manage to do anything?' I asked her.

It was her voice that had answered my call from the bar on the Link Road when I'd told them to get me Room 6.

'Res.' It came out in soft little jerks. 'They're making a priority search – it was reported missing a few minutes before the motorcade started – they needed a little persuading but I – persuaded them.'

She couldn't even stand still. Her nerves had set the whole line of her lean body trembling. Loman had said she was with Mil. 6. They shouldn't have kids like this in their outfit because things were bound to break them up. It was happening now.

I said: 'Are they going to use helicopters? Calling the Army in?'

'It's for them to work in their own way – all I stressed was the importance of watching docks, airports and the land routes to the Laos frontier – '

'Laos?'

'The quickest route to China.'

Loman might know. I would ask him.

I said: 'What have you told Loman?'

'Nothing.'

'What has he told you?'

'Nothing.'

'Where's Room 6?'

'I'll show you.'

It was an effort for her to look away from my face. I followed her out of the corridor and we saw Cole-Verity, the Ambassador, surrounded by flapping minions – a big man still in his ceremonial dress, decorations, gold epaulettes, ashen-faced and half-shouting at them: 'Tell them it's an emergency news blackout – get that mob off the steps and block the switchboard – outgoing calls only. McMahon, come in here and bring Straker with you.' They peeled off as he pushed open a door.

Loman had come up from the other direction and he had the same look in his eyes and I knew now what was wrong with the girl and some of the rage came back –

'For Christ's sake, *someone's* got to do it, haven't they?'

Loman took my arm and we went into Room 6 and he locked the door and I said: 'Thank Christ she's gone.'

They're all the same, they don't like it when they know there's been a killing: even after two world wars they look at you as if it's never been done before: even when they know there's a bump on the programme and you're the louse that's got to do it, they look at you afterwards as if you've just climbed out of a drain.

'How did she know, Loman – how much have you told her? What's a Mil. 6 trollop doing in our bloody woodshed?'

'Sit down and control yourself.'

'You couldn't get rid of her, could you – is she your type or something?'

Stomach full of adrenalin, full of acid, sweating like a pig – a feeling of great age, responsibility, failure and defeat. Getting old, too old for it.

He went on waiting, leaning by the window looking down at his shoes. I went twice round the room looking at nothing and trying to think of a word, one word that would tell him what I thought of his talent as an intelligence director and what I thought of the crowd out there in the Link Road where the water-cart was washing away the blood and what I thought of a mission that had run smash into ruins because we couldn't even handle a monkey-sized Mongolian thug whose answer to everything was a bullet.

There wasn't a word for all that.

'When you're ready,' he said.

His calm helped. The whole of the Embassy was rocking under us but he was calm.

'Did you go down to the Link Road?' I asked him. My voice sounded quiet, maybe the contrast, maybe I'd been shouting.

'Yes.'

'What did you see?'

'I couldn't get near anything, so I arranged for you to meet me here and came along to wait.'

'So you don't know anything.'

'No. Perhaps you will tell me.'

'It was a snatch.'

He came away from the window and by the look on his face I could see that he really hadn't known. He said softly: 'Do you mean the Person is still alive?'

'I tell you, it was a snatch. He was never in the sights. It was the driver they shot.'

In the face of his surprise I felt suddenly in control and for the first time saw the room in detail and took an interest in it because I had to orientate myself, find bearings, relearn the familiar. White paint, frescoed ceiling, blue carpet, company-meeting table, chairs, telephone, ash-trays: a sunny room, hospital-clean, the kind of place you always hope you'll be taken to after the accident. That was, in a way, the way it was.

'Go on,' he said.

'I took action as soon as I knew. It was no good telling Ramin's bunch so I got to a phone and asked for Room 6 and the girl answered. I told her to get a dragnet put out for the ambulance – anyone here could use more pressure than I could – they could make it an Embassy alert call – '

'Ambulance,' Loman said.

It was difficult to remember that in the instant of firing the Husqvarna I had been as ignorant as he was now, and that it was only by going to look at the dead man in the Phra Chula Chedi that I'd been able to see the whole picture.

'They got him away in an ambulance,' I said. 'Look, I'll give you the set-up – *his* set-up – Kuo's. He's moved into the snatch game. The Person wasn't down for killing. Somebody wants him, don't ask me what for. And they've got him. We worked on the premise that he was the target of the Kuo gun and he wasn't. The target was the driver of the Cadillac and he was shot dead precisely where the road curved so that the car would just run straight on into the crowd. Then they did the snatch. You imagine the confusion. Two tons at twenty-five miles an hour ramming into living people. I saw the driver, still at the wheel, and a man slumped in the back – both dead.'

Loman asked: 'How was the other man killed?'

'I don't know. It wasn't with a second shot. Kuo shot once – I'd have heard a second shot. I didn't hear the first one because it was covered by the sound of my own – bound to be because we were both operating within a period of a few seconds and it was a few seconds before I got my hearing back. Even if I'd heard his shot I would have thought it was an echo of mine.'

'Where did he shoot from?'

'Look,' I said impatiently and hit the table with the flat of my hand, 'here's the temple. Here's the condemned building. Link Road between them. Get out of your mind for a minute that the target was the *driver*. Suppose – as we did suppose – that the target was the *Person*. The car is running almost head-on towards the temple and it's a perfect site for a marksman because the visual effective speed is about 5 m.p.h. instead of 25. From the temple you could shoot the Person because he was sitting in the back on a seat raised 9 inches. You couldn't shoot the driver because he was behind the windscreen. You could only shoot someone in the back – *over* the screen. I knew this – it's simple geometry. I didn't question it: but I would have questioned it if I'd known the target was the *driver*.'

'He was here, then, Kuo?' His polished nails flashed in the light as he tapped the table.

'Somewhere in this area, near the condemned building. You could only shoot the driver from behind. Same data: car moving *tail-on*, visual effective speed 5 m.p.h. instead of 25 – and no windscreen in the way.'

He went back to the windows. Maybe it was all he wanted to know. It wasn't all I wanted to tell him.

'For God's sake, Loman, if they'd meant to shoot the Person they'd have done it, shot him cold, and we couldn't have done a thing about it, not a damned *thing* about it, can't you get that?'

I'd lost it again and the room spun and I heard him saying 'He's alive and that's what matters – '

'*Shot him cold in front of our bloody eyes* – '

'You'll have to get over that.' Voice coming closer, talked like a bloody governess. 'There are more things I want to know, Quiller. London will ask for a very full report. Who was the man you – who was the man in the temple?'

'Pox on London.' I'd knocked something over, bits on the blue carpet. An ash-tray.

'Who was the man in the temple?'

Eyes were bright.

The room steadied.

'What? I don't know. The seventh man. Pangsapa told us. A decoy.'

I'd have to watch it. Always a strain knowing you've got to do a bump even when you know it's an overkill and always a strain, by God, when you see the whole mission go smash for all the effort you've made. Brain's got to go on ticking, or you've had it.

'He wasn't one of the original Kuo cell?'

I said: 'No. Kuo uses picked men. He wouldn't waste one. Look, I keep telling you – ' I had to stop and think. 'I haven't told you. Listen, Loman. There are some bits I don't understand yet. I don't suppose they matter.' I found I was sitting in one of the chairs. 'They were on to me very early. Knew I was tagging them. For some reason they didn't do anything about it – that's one of the bits I don't understand. Maybe it was orders from on high – that girl's always talking about China – does that mean anything to you – China?'

'You put his fee at around five hundred thousand pounds,' he said. 'Remember?' He was down on his haunches, arms on his knees, hands folded together, perched in front of me, not letting me get away or think about anything else. 'Only a government could afford that. But I don't know anything about China particularly. They were on to you very early – well?'

'They could have put me in the cross-hairs a dozen times. – I knew that – but when they missed the first few chances I didn't worry any more. Christ, d'you think I'd have stood in front of an open window like that at the Pakchong Hotel with the light on and dark outside? I'd taken damn good care, believe me, before I knew they were letting the chances go. Look, I don't mind what risks I take providing there's – '

'They were on to you very early, you said.'

'All right.' I shut my eyes. 'They weren't certain of me till Kuo went to ground – then I had to show my hand, went into the Lotus Bar, other places, all over the bloody town, brothels, the lot. Then they knew I was interested. But they *still* didn't take a crack at me – you knew that, Loman. When you told me that Mil. 6 was protecting me I asked you what the hell they were meant to be protecting me from – Kuo? You said I wasn't in any danger from Kuo. Dead correct. But I was being a nuisance to them so they began fitting the two missions together, his and mine. They let me pick up their tracks – gave me a man to tag, led me to a hotel, let me tag their car down Rama IV, made a show of being worried when I got into their mirror. I knew where they were going, where they were taking the roll of gold cloth, because I'd haunted the bloody place for days – the Phras Chula Chedi – and they'd seen me haunting it. When I – '

'That isn't sufficient.' He got up from his crouch and walked about a lot. 'You're filling in gaps, making things fit – '

'All right. There's a gap, a big one. But *somehow* they knew my set-up – they knew I was going for an overkill. I've tried till I'm sick to find out *how* they – '

'Don't worry it, Quiller. We'll find out. Go on.'

'I've finished.'

'No, you haven't,'

'Oh for God's sake.'

I got out of the chair and fiddled with the telephone cord. 'I suppose they knifed him, the man in the back. Petrol on fire, people lying crushed under the wheels, you could have got away with anything – '

'They couldn't have planned the fire.'

'No, but the rest was enough.' I twisted the telephone cord, garotting my wrist. 'We don't know how many dead, do we? I think he's a bit of a shit and I'm keeping my gun, the Husqvarna – never know your luck.'

He was standing close to me again. 'I must ask you to make your report a little more precisely. You propose that the Kuo cell – six of them, four operators and two bodyguards – had an ambulance waiting at the spot and brought stretchers ostensibly to remove the dead and injured, and that in the confusion they knifed the guard in the royal car, knocked the Person down – '

'Hit him behind the knees, rabbit-punch as he fell – '

'And took him to the ambulance with a blanket over him, and drove off.'

'Tell me how else they did it.' The cord had left a weal on my wrist.

'It was probably like that. The police couldn't have reached the scene – the immediate scene – in time to realize what was happening, and those in the car wouldn't have gone on sitting there like dummies, with people all round them in agony – they would have climbed from the car to help, even knowing that their driver had been shot dead. It was a nightmare, the perfect setting for an abduction.'

'The cell would have trained for weeks. He's a professional. Listen Loman, how much chance have we got of – '

'What I would like you to do is to pick up where you left off. You say that they laid a false trail for you, letting you see the gun being delivered to the temple, and letting you see Kuo himself at the oriel more than once. I take you to mean that? You said they began fitting the two missions together.'

'Tell me how *else* – '

'Oh, I accept most of what you say. It's glaringly logical. I am only trying to help you complete the picture.'

'Well that's it.' His calmness was beginning to stink.

The mission was over and it had failed but the Person hadn't been shot dead so everything was all right now and Loman could go home and make his report.

'Tell London,' I said. 'And don't forget the cost of the drawing-pins or they won't sleep.'

'To continue,' he said equably, 'you believe they set up a decoy for you, a live dummy you could shoot at, the "seventh man" who joined the cell late. Why?'

'To keep me out of their way – to stop me finding out their real set-up – to keep me busy fiddling while the whole of bloody Rome was burning down – '

'Why? Why did they want to keep you busy – to keep you *alive*, instead of killing you off in the early stages?'

'How the hell do I know?' We were facing each other without meaning to, both of us wandering round the damned room looking at nothing, coming up against each other.

'Perhaps you were wanted, too. As well as the Person.'

I stared at him.

'Then why didn't they come and get me?'

'Perhaps they will,' he said.

Chapter Sixteen

NEWSBREAK

I went on staring at him.

'*Now?* But it's over, for God's sake. They've made a perfect snatch.'

He turned away with distaste. 'In view of the Person's standing I do wish you would refer to it as an abduction.'

My laugh exploded, unreal, like the squawk of a mechanical doll. 'Abduction . . .' I said, 'abduction . . .' trying to make sense of the word. 'Listen, what would they want *me* for? Bumping that thug – the decoy? He was just a hired tool, a live dummy set up as a target for me. You think he meant anything to Kuo? There must have been ten killed in that crowd and the decoy meant as little to Kuo as any of them – '

'Do you *really* believe' – he swung round on me suddenly – 'that they would have set up such an *elaborate* device to prevent your defeating their mission unless *someone* had given the most express orders that your life was not to be taken? Haven't you admitted that they could have killed you time and time again?'

'All right, but *now*?'

He didn't answer and I had time to think. It had all gone so damned fast and there were things I hadn't been able to see – things in the background that had formed the overall pattern while all I could think of was getting my eye in the Balvar sight and my finger on the tit.

'Listen to me, Quiller.'

The room seemed to have gone cold and my head was clearing as if a fever were dying out. The thing had looked so big because the Person was involved. Was there something bigger beyond it? This was why the Bureau made it a rule: the intelligence director tries to ensure that his agent in the field is left free of all information that doesn't directly concern his mission. The ferret is sent into the hole and he is not told about the dog at the other end.

'Listen to me,' he said again. 'You have been concentrating on a very limited and very calculated operation. You have had no time to think beyond the simple mechanics. That is understandable. Before long you'll realize there's a very big question left in the air: *why* has the Person been abducted?'

I'd never thought about it and he knew it and left me hooked on it because it was important for me to get it into my head, or he wouldn't have sprung it. After a bit he went on.

'I have made little or no contact here with the official Embassy staff or with the fringe groups operating under its aegis. Vinia Maine has told me nothing about her cell or about her mission. But one picks up signs here and there and for your information I would say this: Mil. 6 is running a special operation the subject of which is yourself. You have been under close observation and protection since you flew in from Paris. You will remain under observation and protection until the Kuo mission is completed, and that won't be until the Person has left Thailand – still under restraint and duress. The Kuo cell has taken great pains to see that you stay alive and they haven't done that for humanitarian reasons. Or do you think so?'

I thought of the water-cart busily cleaning up.

'Not really, no.'

He suddenly began speaking softly and urgently:

'The Ambassador is now back from the Link Road, as you know. He was on the spot when the Person was abducted and he will by now have heard that your signal to Room 6 has alerted the police. He will follow that up very hard. Further, in a few hours when the news blackout is lifted the bombshell will burst over England – the news that the Person is missing and believed to be in danger. Enormous pressure will be brought to bear on Thailand to redeem its failure in protecting a most distinguished visitor. The hunt will be mounted on a vast scale.'

He paused and I said nothing. My head was now perfectly lucid: the feverish residue of a concentrated, inept and mucky operation had found its own level and my subconscious would have to deal with it as best it could. Brain-think was again available.

Loman's bright stare was on me and his hands beat the air like trapped birds as he drummed into me the importance of what he was saying.

'Kuo will know what he is up against. He won't have come to Bangkok without having made the most meticulous plans to get out again – with his prisoner. His mission will be completed only when the Person has been transferred from Thailand to the soil of whatever country mounted that mission and hired Kuo to perform it. He will almost certainly have to lie low in a pre-arranged place, here in this city, with his cell and with his prisoner, for days or even weeks while the hunt passes overhead. That will have been an alternative plan.'

He turned away and when he spoke again I knew why. He didn't like buttering up lice to their face.

'It will console you to know that I call it an *alternative* plan because he had probably counted on fast and immediate clearance, which is no longer open to him. It is unlikely that anyone would have realized that one of the 'dead' bodies taken to the ambulance was in fact the Person's. There would have been ample time for that ambulance to reach a private airfield and take off for the frontier. Your call to Room 6 prevented it. Ambulances carry radio and this one – which was almost certainly stolen – would have monitored the police-patrol radio system. They will have already heard of the search and will have gone to ground as the prearranged alternative to flying out.'

He made a tour of the room and came up behind me and I didn't turn round so he had to pass me and turn himself and face me again. The compliments were over and we were both pleased.

'The point is this, Quiller. Until such time as the Kuo cell can get their prisoner to a frontier their mission is still running. And your situation is unchanged. From the signs I have picked up I think you'll remain under the observation and protection of Mil. 6, so that *their* mission is still running. They are a rival group but we know they are far from idiots.'

Watching me, he began nodding and his tone lost its headlong urgency. 'You already see the point. The Kuo cell has so far left you alone and left you alive – though of course I'm not saying you couldn't have survived any attack, as an experienced agent should be able. But up to now Mil. 6 has thought that there is good reason for your having been – shall we say – preserved. And as long as you are of interest to the Kuo cell and to their operations, *our* mission is still running. And it won't finish until we know why the Person has been abducted, and why you appear to be linked with him as a subject for preservation. It won't finish until we can restore him to safety if everyone else fails. Or until we too fail.'

He left me again, going to the windows.

Vaguely I listened to the sounds outside the room: bells, doors slamming, voices. They were sounds of disorderliness and I was angry because I could have prevented all this and the bombshell that would soon break over England and the mess that the water-cart had been clearing away.

'How much did you already know, Loman?'

His short body looked black, silhouetted against the glare of the window. He didn't turn round.

'I had a lot of pieces, but they wouldn't fit. They would have fitted the theory of an abduction, but we didn't consider that. Why should anyone abduct him? But now most of it fits. Most of it.'

'One thing I want to know. How did they find out my set-up? How did they know I was going to try for an overkill?'

'That is not for you to worry.'

I thought of Pangsapa again. It didn't add up. Pangsapa had given us the motorcade route and he had told us that a seventh man had joined the Kuo cell. I might even have seen the light: a seventh man could mean a decoy.

The telephone had started to ring and Loman answered it. I looked round the room again, seeing things I'd missed before: two desks, a typewriter, tape-recorder, wall-safe.

'I will see,' he said, and pressed a switch for one of the internal lines. 'Miss Maine? There's a call for you.'

Before she came in I said: 'I thought they were blocking incoming calls.'

'Mil. 6 has a special line'. He began moving towards the door and I thought it would be a good thing when the Bureau realized that an important facility for any mission is a decent Local Control. I was getting fed up with gem-shops, kite-sheds and rooms we had to be chucked out of whenever the phone rang.

She came in and looked at Loman, not me.

'Please stay. I shan't disturb you for more than a few minutes.' She went to the telephone.

Loman hesitated. I asked him:

'What *is* Room 6?'

He decided it would be difficult to shepherd me out. 'It's a clearing-house for those groups not on the official Embassy staff, but for all practical purposes it belongs to Mil. 6. Hence the number.'

All she was saying on the phone was yes and no. They were doing the talking. I asked Loman: 'Why the hell should Mil. 6 lend us a facility?'

Patiently he said: 'Is there a better way of making sure they can maintain contact with us, since you are the subject under their protection?'

'Why did you let them do it?'

'When an organization of good repute offers protection to one of my agents I don't refuse. You may one day profit from that.'

He was listening to her too but there was nothing useful. She must have known what kind of call it was or she wouldn't have asked us to stay while she took it.

I looked at her once and in that same second she looked back at me. To break it up I asked Loman: 'Why isn't the Cultural Attaché ever in his office?'

'He's there most of the time but he lets her bring people through there so that they can be vetted when necessary.'

'He must spend a lot of his time in the lav.'

'Don't forget,' Loman said, 'that they have more facilities than we do. They exist.'

When she put the phone down we weren't talking.

She said: 'The first news has just gone out over Radio Thailand.'

Loman was attentive. 'Then it's a world-wide release.'

She smiled faintly. 'It had to happen some time.' With an oblique glance at me she said: 'The ambulance has been found abandoned. It was reported as having a radio fault about an hour before the motorcade left the Palace – no one could get an acknowledgement. Half an hour later it was reported stolen. Now it's been found. The crew were shot dead and dumped into the Klong Maha Nak, after their uniforms had been taken.'

She was moving round so that the left side of her face was away from the windows. Loman asked:

'Is there a search mounted?'

'Oh yes.' She looked at him as if he ought to have known. 'Everyone's in – the Metro Police, Special Branch, CID, Auxiliary Services, Crime Suppression Division radio and anti-riot units.

Even the Army – the King issued an emergency decree. Commando units are recalled to barracks.'

She was repeating what they'd been telling her on the phone and I got fed up and said: 'Look, is your outfit going to keep on getting in my way?'

Loman looked upset and I felt better.

She moved towards me a bit, head poised at an angle on the slender neck. The eyes still flickered sometimes but she didn't look at me any more as if I were Frankenstein's pet.

'We don't want to lose you,' she said.

'You'll have to. I'm going to ground.'

I don't know what I would have said if Loman hadn't been with us. Other things. Or the same thing in other ways.

She said quietly: 'We shall still do what we can. It's important.'

It wasn't clever and I shouldn't have tried it but I couldn't stop half-way once I'd started. 'Any particular reason?'

I saw Loman go poker-faced.

She said: 'Yes. We know why the abduction was made. Do you?'

Chapter Seventeen

LEE

The city was under siege.

Road-blocks had been set up at all major points of exit manned by units of the Royal Thai Army. Traffic attempting to leave the city had to pass through a bottle-neck of tank-traps, machine-gun posts and barbed wire in depth. Outward passage was permitted only after credentials had been examined by teams from the Bangkok Special Branch and all vehicles rigorously searched.

Passenger coaches serving the eighteen international airlines operating through Don Muang Airport were given mobile police escort through the road-blocks after each passenger was examined and screened at the airline offices in the heart of the city. Bus, train and road services were interrupted and all travellers entering Bangkok were warned that there would be serious delays before they could be permitted emergency exit-passes.

Units of the US Special Forces permanently stationed in the country had been drafted into the area following the immediate acceptance of an offer by the US Government to place certain troops and facilities at the service of the Thai Army. Infantry search-parties were linked across the rice-field areas working in radio-liaison with military helicopters flying a non-stop schedule.

Sea-going traffic moving southwards down the Chao Phraya River was caught in the dragnet set up by naval gunboats on the north side of Kratumban. All ships were searched by auxiliary units of the River Police. Inland from Bangkok the river was blockaded on the south side of Nontaburi with a machine-gun post on each bank and a group of armed inspection-vessels patrolling the mid-stream lanes.

A ring of armed guards was drawn round Don Muang and every other airfield in the southern provinces and the owners of all private aeroplanes were ordered by special emergency decrees to immobilize their machines by draining the fuel tanks and removing the distributor rotors, and to report immediately any attempt by strangers to approach hangars or mooring-areas.

In the besieged city the flags had been taken down. Five thousand police drawn from the North and South Bangkok Metropolitan and auxiliary forces had begun a systematic search of every room in every building in every street. Mobile patrols cruised on a round-the-clock schedule covering a search-pattern specially devised by the city traffic-control planners. All crews were armed.

Theatres, cinemas and dance-halls had closed and few people dined out. There was no music by night. The gold domes of the temples stood among silent trees. The city was numbed by the shock of the realization that its streets were not safe, by fear for its missing guest and by grief for its dead.

Fourteen people had lost their lives when the royal car plunged into the crowd; by nightfall three of the injured had died. A memorial service had already been arranged to take place in the Palace grounds on the day following the tragedy.

News of world reaction reached the city hourly by radio and cable. Little news went out.

'Naturally it will prove ineffective,' Pangsapa said to me. 'An effort must be seen to be made, and anxiety for the safety of so distinguished a person must be expressed, therefore they are throwing whole armies into the search. Well and good. But ineffective.'

He had signalled me through the Embassy before I'd left Room 6 and I had come straight to his house because I was ready to snatch at any straw, any bit of information from anyone at all that might give me a direction to follow.

I said 'You think they've still got him here in the city.'

'Of course.'

He sat in his black robe on the cushions and there was incense burning somewhere and I felt I had come to Delphi. Inaction when action is most desperately needed begets false hopes. I didn't think Pangsapa had anything I could use.

'The nearest airfield is an hour's drive,' I said.

'Too far. They had no time to reach it in the ambulance before the hunt was up and they had no time to switch vehicles. They're still here in the city and you could deploy all the troops and aeroplanes in Asia quite ineffectively. Armies need room to move. The police may have better luck among the cellars and the ruined temples and the riverside wharves. But there are only two people in the whole city with any real hope of finding the man you so discreetly call "the Person". I refer to our two selves.'

Today something was different about him, about his eyes or voice or the way he sat, and I couldn't even name this difference but it was there. I began watching him more carefully.

'In your case,' he said, his tone slightly sing-song, 'you know Kuo and his cell better than anyone in the whole of Bangkok, because the police observed them for a few days and they did it in shifts, whereas you made a study of them and you worked alone. You had, after all, certain intentions towards Kuo, and these necessitated your observing him with far greater care than the police.' The topaz-yellow eyes did not glance in my direction. (Question: how much did he know?) 'In my case,' he went on in the same slightly lilting tone, 'I possess information sources which the police would find it difficult to tap, since they spring from what is called the "underworld".' Plaintively he added: 'I don't know why the word should always refer to cities. Every man has his own underworld and a part of him never leaves it.'

The difference was revealing itself in his eyes, voice and posture, but I still couldn't name it, quite.

'However that may be, we make a formidable team, Mr Quiller. We have an enormous advantage. It would be a pity to waste it.' Leaning towards me suddenly, he said, 'It is essential that we keep in close contact. I have people working for me now, at this moment, working for *us*. They are questioning those whom the police cannot question – at least with any hope of a straight answer – and they are searching places of which the police have no knowledge at all. I cannot tell you when I shall have information for you. It may be tomorrow. It may be five minutes after you have left my house.'

Nerves. The name of the difference that was in him today. He was showing nerves: when the eyes moved they moved quickly; the English university speech-forms were remembered with less ease and the Asian lilt and the lisp were beyond his control; the stillness of the Lotus pose was irksome to him – the limbs wanted to express the speed of thought that drove his mind. Pangsapa was nervous.

I could see no reason.

'So my question is obvious,' he said. 'How and where can I contact you with *immediacy*?'

Just as there is calculated risk there is calculated trust and sometimes they are the same thing. There was a calculated risk in trusting Pangsapa and it was worth taking. This kind of thing nearly always happens towards the end of a mission: you move into increasingly dangerous areas because the risks you must take become greater. The adverse party has been seen and marked down and he knows it and is provoked and you are yourself marked down because he too is fiercely determined to survive.

But you cannot both survive.

'The Pakchong,' I told Pangsapa.

The Link Road thing had happened only a few hours ago and I was homeless and my time in the condemned building was at an end. Mil. 6 knew a dozen places now where they could pick me up until I went to ground and the Pakchong might just as well be one of them. It would be amusing for a night or two to sleep like a gentleman in a bed.

'You won't always be there,' he said.

'Loman will know where I am.'

'And if Mr Loman is not at that number?' He meant Room 6 and was careful not to say it.

'I think that about covers it.' I wasn't giving him Soi Suek 3.

'Would I have permission to contact you through Mr Varaphan?'

I didn't answer. I'd taken care – nothing showed in my face. He would expect surprise but I didn't want him to see actual shock.

A safe-house is no ordinary place: it is a cornerstone of security and bad security can wreck a mission and kill you off. You've got Local Control if you're lucky but you can't always rely on getting there if the operation hots up and you're jumping. A safe-house is a home and sometimes it's the only place you can run to. We think of it as a shrine, sacrosanct. It's really a bolt-hole.

'How did you get it, Pangsapa?'

Because he'd got it and it was no use asking him who Mr Varaphan was. He knew.

I had never seen anger in him before. There wasn't much difference: he sat as still, and didn't raise his voice. Anger in an Asian is no more – and no less – than sudden cold.

'Please remember that Mr Loman gave you my name and that he gave you also Varaphan's. How much do you trust in your own intelligence director?' His yellow eyes remained fixed on me.

I said: 'Let's say, then, that you can contact me at the Pakchong, through Loman, or through Varaphan.'

My own anger didn't show either. Loman hadn't given it to him. I knew that. A safe-house didn't have that name for nothing. Pangsapa must have tags out. That was unusual. He was an informant, and informants are not active. They are found among newsvendors and clerks, maîtres-d'hôtel, cloth-importers, stockbrokers and road-sweepers – they can be anyone. They are businessmen who listen and who buy and sell what they hear, and they trade outside their ordinary occupation.

They don't put tags out.

Kuo was a professional killer but he had moved into the snatch game. Pangsapa was a narcotics contrabandist and an informant on the side. Now he was on the move. And *that* was why he was different today and why his nerves were poking through the black silk and the Lotus pose and the lilt in his speech.

He lisped carefully: 'I gave you the motorcade route. I gave you the man who joined Kuo. I can give you more. It is up to you whether you are prepared to take your advantage.'

'I'm ready to take everything I can get. You still don't mention the price.'

'Why should I? It is not you who will have to pay.'

I had walked half a block from Pangsapa's house when the car began slowing behind me and I caught the sound and turned sharply to face it because that is the only chance you can give yourself – to look straight at the car, at the windows on the pavement side.

The reflections of the streetlamps went sliding across the metal roof. I watched it coming. The windows on my side were open but nothing protruded. The driver was alone.

She reached across and opened the passenger door as the car stopped and I got in without saying anything. She drove easily, taking her time along the empty streets. The cinemas and most of the restaurants were dark and the only patch of light along Charoen Krung Road was made by the police-station, where patrol-crews were assembled for rebriefing under floodlights. We were slowed and a man looked in and then nodded, waving us on.

It was all they could do: check everyone, search every house, question everything they saw. They had no direction, any more than I had. They would have asked for statements from people who had been at the scene and they would have drawn blank because no one can remember anything after an accident: knowing that one is expected to remember, one rationalizes and puts up a show to avoid being thought a half-wit. The testimony is worse than useless because it is unconsciously false.

They would have extracted the bullet from the head of the dead driver and again they would have drawn blank because they'd never find the gun that had fired it. Kuo was a professional. They would have asked to see anyone who had been using a camera at the time and they would have drawn blank because there was no point in studying amateur photographs of a car hitting a crowd. The press photographers had been bunched in special enclosures and there had been no enclosure in the Link Road. Blank.

Even from my raised viewpoint in the condemned building I had seen nothing clearly, even with field-glasses.

But they had to go on trying because routine work by massed forces will sometimes repay the effort. At worst the effort is seen to be made.

South Sathorn Road with the Klong running parallel on our left. There were no rings on her hands; they were cool-looking and long-fingered, tenderly moving on the hard rim of the wheel. Sometimes her reflection came against the screen, a ghost face flying along the street's façade.

It was too late now to do anything about it. The tricks wouldn't work any more – calling her a bitch, calling her Scarface, resenting her, telling Loman to get her out of my way. Loman had seen the signs: he had said, 'That's the second time you've mentioned her.' I should have shut up there and then.

North Sathorn, passing the Immigration Office. We were heading for the Pakchong Hotel, my last known address before I'd gone to ground and she'd lost me for three days. Didn't she bloody well have anywhere else to go? It didn't work any more. I didn't want her to have anywhere else to go.

Near Lumpini Park a police-patrol was throwing a man into the van; he ducked once and nearly got clear enough to start running, then they chopped him short and picked him up and threw him in; one of his shoes had been wrenched off and they threw it in after him. He was one of hundreds; the cells were crammed with suspects held for questioning since the search was mounted.

Vithayu Road, turning north. Far over to the left a beam of light stood against the dark sky, tapering upwards: a helicopter probing along the river.

The night was warm and her arms were bare. She must have tagged me from the Embassy when I'd left there to answer Pangsapa's call; then she had waited for me to come out of his house. I had been there for nearly an hour and she had used the time thinking, sitting alone in the car, undistracted, thinking it all out.

Then she had decided, and picked me up. Until now we had driven in silence through the city, leaving each other in peace.

Her head lifted a fraction but she didn't turn to look at me.

'Do you remember,' she said, 'a man named Lee? Norwich, England, July last year?'

And I knew why Kuo had made the snatch.

Chapter Eighteen

THE SWOP

The maximum sentence that can be imposed on a foreign national convicted of espionage in the United Kingdom is fourteen years, and the man calling himself Peter Lee had received this term at the hands of the Lord Chief Justice in No. 1 Court, Old Bailey, in July 1965.

The real name of the prisoner was Huang Hsiung Lee and the affair became known as the Norwich Case. A group of distinguished physicists headed by Sir Arthur Hare and Professor James K. W. Fadieman had been working on a project for two years at Norwich Physical Research Establishment under a special Treasury grant and with certain technical facilities provided by the USA, three of whose scientists were among the team. The project concerned a refinement of the Laser device (Light Amplification by Stimulate Emission of Radiation). This is an electro-magnetic oscillator producing light-waves massed into an ultra-narrow wave-length band and directed along a fixed path in a ray one million times brighter than is possible in any normal way.

The Laser beam has been used successfully in surgery of the eye, operating at a distance of a few inches. A beam directed by the same method at the surface of the planet Venus at a distance of 23 million miles has been reflected back to Earth and picked up by optic receptors. Between these two extreme instances of its remarkable range the Laser has capabilities that make it essential that strict security covers all research into its further development.

Data produced by the Hare-Fadieman Project during those two years had automatically passed on to the secret list. MI5 and the CIA set up a special unit to protect every aspect of the Norwich research, but in January 1965 an agent seconded to the technical branch of a UK mission in Teheran intercepted a signal concerning an entirely different subject and triggered a snap-enquiry that sent a Special Branch car to No. 67 Beacon Street, Norwich, within twenty-four hours. 'Peter' Lee, a student in applied physics with friends at the Research Establishment, was arrested and charged with being in possession of information coming under the Secrets Act.

A second and immediate enquiry among the Hare-Fadieman research team established that the leak was of the most serious proportions. On the same day an exhaustive search of Lee's apartment in Beacon Street revealed microdot photographs of two comprehensive files and third-phase technical drawings on the subject of a stage in the development of the Laser instrument so far in advance of its current potential that any government on a war-footing would take the most extreme measures to possess its raw data.

Further enquiries revealed that 'Peter' Lee, whose family was in Singapore, had recently asked permission to curtail his studies at Norwich owing to his father's illness. He had planned to leave England three days after the Teheran signal had set in motion the enquiries. At the time of his arrest he had been in the process of settling small local bills, and one of his travel-cases was already packed.

At the trial in July the Lord Chief Justice had made a point of congratulating those agents responsible for the action, and public opinion swung from alarm at the first news of the leak to re-assurance that it had been stopped in time, by however fine a limit. The microdot material had been destroyed and Lee was sent down for the maximum term. He could do no further damage. The Norwich Case was closed.

The streetlamps swung overhead, their light throwing the reflection of her face against the windscreen. I watched it as it brightened and faded block after block.

I said: 'Where are you dropping me?'

She said: 'Nowhere.' I knew what she meant.

'I've got some things to pick up at the warehouse.' She knew where it was: the place where she had tagged Loman and opened a door to listen, the night when – knowing she was listening – I had called her Scarface.

Lee. I thought about him. The public had been reassured, and only a few people had gone on worrying. I was one of those. We knew that Huang Hsiung Lee had an intellectual quality that came very high on the list among technical operators: he had a brilliant and photographic memory.

It didn't matter, so long as he was in prison.

It mattered now.

'A straight swop,' I said.

She said: 'Yes.'

'But they can't do it. It can't be on government level.' I suddenly felt annoyed. 'No government can admit they've ordered a snatch on *this* scale, with someone as big as the Person.'

She was silent.

I said: 'They can't play outside the rules. A spy for a spy. They can't just – '

The sensation was almost physical: bright light flooding into my head.

You light your lamps as you go, picking your way through the dark . . . There are patches of dark and you skirt them, because your lamps are too small to show you everything . . . Now she had thrown a floodlight across the whole area and for a minute I was blinded.

In the reflection of her face the eyes had moved; she was watching the reflection of my own. She said:

'That's right, Quill. It's a straight swop. But if they can't get him to the frontier, they'll get you.'

I remembered Loman: 'Our mission is still running, and it won't finish until we know why the Person has been abducted, and why you appear to be linked with him as a subject for preservation.'

I said to her: 'That's why they held off, why they didn't try putting me in the sights.'

'Yes. You're the reserve – a substitute if they can't get him to the frontier.'

We turned back through Lumpini Park on the way to the kite warehouse and I asked her to pull up under the trees. Over to our right was the haze-grey jet of the fountain. They had turned the lights off; normally it was illuminated but tonight its gaiety would not become the city.

She moved in her seat and her face had all the warmth the reflection had lacked. I knew she would talk now because she'd already given me the central picture. I said:

'When did your group come in?'

'Some weeks ago.' She no longer spoke in nervous snatches. Her eyes were cool and steady, as they'd been when I had first seen her in the Cultural Attaché's office. The flickering had gone. 'We got a lead from one of our people in Hong Kong that an attempt was going to be made to spring Lee from Durham. No one in London could confirm – they said we must have duff info. But we kept checking and found it was right: Lee was down for exchange. The only snag was that the Chinese Republic didn't have a candidate. There was no one to exchange for Lee. We knew they'd have to find someone and that he'd have to be someone fairly big. Then we got wind that your Bureau was sending a protection man to deal with the assassination threat. We knew it was likely to be you because of your work in Bangkok two years ago – you know this place blindfold. So we set up a protection mission of our own. You were looking after the Person – we were going to look after you.'

I glanced away through the windscreen because I wanted to think with a cold forebrain. I said:

'You didn't think it was the Person himself up for a swop.'

She said impatiently: 'Did you?'

'I just wondered. Mil. 6 can be a bloody nuisance but it works. Who sent the threat?'

I was hoping to ask her something she didn't know. Rivalry is insidious. Mil. 5, Mil. 6, the FBI and the CIA – they're at each other's throats trying to do the same job in the same way. You find yourself caught up in it. No excuse.

'The threat was sent by a Thai who had picked up a clue by accident. He'd heard that Kuo the Mongolian was coming to Bangkok. He chose the safest way to tip off London – anonymously. Kuo is very much feared, and you don't sign your name to information against him.'

Headlights swept the lawns and flower-beds and a police-van pulled up quietly near the fountain. Another followed and they doused their lights. I asked her:

'Why did you have me checked when I showed up at the Embassy?'

'I wasn't sure of you. I'd never seen you before.' She watched the vans too. 'As soon as you were identified without any doubt my group knew the mission was on. From that minute we never lost sight of you except when you – took evasive action.'

Ten uniformed police, five from each van, made a ring and closed in on the fountain. Under the great jet there was a flower-covered blockhouse with a small iron door. It was where the pump was installed. I said without wanting to:

'But you lost sight of me this morning. When the motorcade began. You didn't know where I was.'

Her voice became tremulous again, just by a degree. 'We knew you were holed up in the Link Road area.' It seemed that she was going to leave it at that. The ring of police had reached the small iron door. She said: 'They have found the man in the Phra Chula Chedi – in the temple – did you know?'

It must have been the three priests who had been at the gates. They had wanted to know what I'd been doing in there. I looked at her again and saw the faint flickering of the eyes. I asked her:

'How much did you know about my set-up?'

'We knew you had to . . . shield the Person in the only way possible.'

I looked back to the fountain. She wanted me to talk but there was nothing interesting to say about the man in the Phra Chula Chedi. The police had opened the small iron door and searched the pump-house and were coming back to the vans. It was going on throughout the city but they wouldn't find him. Kuo wouldn't go to earth in any obvious place like a ruin or a wharf or a fountain pump-house.

'How long,' I asked her, 'have you been in the trade?'

Perhaps it wasn't just that death had a fascination for her; perhaps she was unused to it.

'Three years, on active ops.'

'Mil. 6 all the time?'

'Except for the Karachi show.'

I looked at her; she was watching the police. I said: "63?'

'Yes.' She still didn't turn her head.

The Bureau hadn't been in on that show because it amounted to an almost military operation including an air-drop and briefing liaison with the Pakistani opposite numbers and we hadn't enough operators free. It was successful but very messy and it might have been after that mission that she'd had to undergo plastic surgery. Three people – two of them Mil. 6 – had got killed. Davis, Chandler, Browne. No, it wasn't that she was unused to death. Then why the morbid interest in one dead duck?

A couple of policemen were coming across to vet us. They had their right hands loose against the hip, just over the holster.

'Who was your chief in that field?' I asked her.

'Karachi?' She still wouldn't look at me. There was answer enough in the slight jerk of her head. 'I forget.'

They ordered me out of the car and checked our papers with flashlamps, double-checking with a few questions about the Embassy staff before they stood back politely and gave us a salute. They went across to their vans and I got into the car again.

She started up and we drove out of Lumpini, because I didn't want to talk about the man in the temple and she didn't want to talk about the Karachi thing. It is a commonplace that once a sensitive subject comes up in a conversation, reference to anything in the world will somehow lead back to it.

We turned right into Rama IV and headed for the Link Road and I reviewed a final thought about Lee. At the time of his trial he had been called a 'brilliant and perceptive student' by his mentors and it was fairly certain that his studies were a cover. Therefore the data and drawings contained in the microphoto-graphed material were probably within his range of under-standing. This fact, taken together with his excellent memory, meant that he still carried valuable information on Laser de-velopment in his head. Overlapping this factor was a second probability: that he would have taken duplicate copies in micro-dot for his own keeping in case it were unsafe to transmit the others, or in case there were a risk of their being lost in tran-sit.

The Republic of China, determined to take its place among the power-elite of nations, possessed no decisive weapon of war. A refinement of the Laser ray, turned to hostile use, could provide that country with the power to threaten, a power far greater than the fission bomb that nobody dared throw.

Their most brilliant agent, Huang Hsiung Lee, must have got one signal through to Peking before he was arrested. He must have told his Control that he was in possession of valuable material. They knew what he had been looking for; they had then known that he had got it. From that moment they must have set up a priority ways-and-means committee entrusted with one task: to get Lee home. At whatever cost.

The warehouse stood dark against the stars.

'Which door?' she asked.

'The one in the alley.'

All I took was the overnight case. The rest of the stuff was too well concealed to worry about.

We were stopped twice on the way to the Pakchong Hotel by police-patrols and I knew it must be even more difficult on the routes out of the city that led to the road-blocks. Bangkok was a trap.

The same room at the hotel was still reserved for me; I had made a point of that because it wasn't easy to find anywhere: the Person's visit had filled the town. I had the travel-case sent up and we took the stairs while the night-porter was still in the lift.

We had nothing to say to each other; it was now too urgent for that. In the glow from the bedside lamp she moved without awkwardness, revealing her lean body with feline arrogance until she was naked except for the wafer-flat ·22 that was holstered on the inside of her thigh. She unclipped it deftly and dropped it on to her clothes.

Chapter Nineteen

HALFMASK

She had cried out, the first time, and afterwards the heat of her tears touched my hand. She had said his name – *Richard* – without meaning to, without knowing it.

Davis, Chandler, Browne. One of them.

God grant that the dead can be consoled.

We had both wanted the light, and then I had turned it off at last in the early hours of the morning. We had both slept but I was awake again.

The phosphorous dial said 3.21 a.m. The animal is easily satisfied; the encephalon is more demanding. My head felt clear and thought had begun streaming through it because questions had to be answered.

Question: Had the decoy known he was going to die? Doubtful. Suicide missions were a wartime phenomenon, even among Orientals. No, he had been put up like a clay pipe, expendable. Probable mechanics: he was recruited by cash and told that he was to be a reserve. His orders were to take over the sniping-post set up by Kuo, to man it in readiness and to shoot into the royal car *once it had passed the curve*. If it passed the curve it would mean that Kuo had shot and missed or had jammed his gun or was for some reason holding his fire and leaving the kill for his reserve.

It was the decoy's photograph I had taken, unless he had shown himself in the oriel only within the final hour before the motorcade when Kuo had had to make for his own post. Care would have been taken that there was a reasonable likeness; the smoked glasses were the finishing touch; the heat-haze was taken into account, also the range.

Question: How had Kuo known my set-up? Loman had told me not to worry that one. Nevertheless I worried.

Question: Why had a distinguished VIP been chosen for the exchange? An ordinary businessman – Wynne – had been a good enough swop for Lonsdale. Answer: It was getting too easy. If the practice of exchanging captured agents were to become common it would give rise to a grossly dangerous situation: agents would take absurd risks to get hold of information, knowing that (in the UK) a fourteen-year sentence would be cut short the moment a candidate for exchange was available. The greater the risk taken, the greater the chances of seizing the information required. On these terms every major Power would be tempted to build up and maintain an exchange pool so that the moment an agent was caught he could be flown home – with his valuable information fresh in his head or in microdots smaller than a grain of rice concealed on him. Innocent tourists would no longer be safe in any country whose exchange pool was running low: a trumped-up charge of 'suspicious behaviour' would be enough to hold a man indefinitely as a future exchange candidate.

In the case of Huang Hsiung Lee it was known that he had gained access to material of the highest value to a potential enemy and for this reason Peking had been forced to extreme measures. Their candidate had to be someone for whom the UK was prepared to surrender even such a prize as the Hare-Fadieman Project discovery.

Question: How could any government admit that it had ordered the blatant abduction of a distinguished person and had entrained the slaughter of innocent citizens during the operation? It was a deliberate act of violence. Greville Wynne and others had been held on charges of espionage. Abduction of a person against whom no such charge could be made – even falsely – was a new dimension.

The thought persisted, uncertain of itself: this couldn't be on government level. But Loman and Vinia both knew more than I.

Loman: 'Who can afford a sum like that? Only a government.'

Vinia: 'I thought you might be getting on a plane ... You can't cross into China.'

Vinia again: 'If they can't get him to the frontier, they'll get you.' She had meant the Chinese frontier.

End of questions. They weren't important. The mission was still running. Target: locate the Kuo cell and get the Person out of their hands with a whole skin before the UK was forced into an exchange that would spring Lee and surrender a super-weapon to a Communist State that would turn it immediately against the free world.

Sounds rose from the street through the insect-screens at the windows: a car pulling up, challenged by a patrol. It was cleared and drove off.

One question above all: Where was Kuo? Somewhere in this city, in this trap. Making his plans to get out and take his prisoner with him. Kuo the Mongolian had pulled off a major snatch in full daylight and in the presence of massed police and bodyguard protection. A simple road-block wouldn't stop him now.

'Is it morning?'

The sound of the car had wakened her or she had been awake for some time and I hadn't known.

'It's nearly four,' I said.

She slid from me and stood for a minute looking down and in the faint light from the street I saw that she was smiling. 'It feels like morning. It feels like the morning after a lifetime.'

I put the lamp on before she came back from the bathroom. She saw the gun in my hand.

'It's not for show,' she said quietly.

I had picked it up to admire it, never having seen a gun so flat. It was an Astra Cub, a 12-ounce miniature with a 3-inch barrel, potent at short range. The special holster was exquisitely designed, adding no more than one-eighth to the thickness.

'I don't imagine so,' I said, and gave it to her.

'It's for killing.' Clipping it against her thigh, she looked up at me through the silky fall of her hair. Her voice had gone cold and I knew that before we had made love she wouldn't have told me this but that she was going to tell me now. 'I want to apologize, Quill.'

I said nothing.

The little gun was beautiful but against her slim thigh it was a hideous disfigurement.

'I said his name aloud,' she told me. 'I remember doing it. At those times we . . . often say things. It was because you were so . . . magnificent. I forgot where I was, who you were.'

She began dressing. I said:

'I never heard you.'

She glanced her thanks. 'His name was Richard and I was with him when they shot him dead through both his eyes.' She spoke very fast, very softly. 'I don't know who "they" were – they were just the enemy – but they could have done it some other way, couldn't they – not through the eyes. Of course it's not really important – you remember people as they were not as they were when they died. But they needn't have done it in front of me – and they needn't have done it like that.'

Her dress was on and she lifted her hands, drawing back her hair, shutting her eyes for a second to blot out the scene she had made herself remember; then her hands came down and smoothed the dress over her hips. 'Look,' she said softly. 'Nothing shows. But it's there, and it's for killing.'

And suddenly I remembered. It was one of those stories that do the rounds – you hear it first in a pub in the Strand and a different version in a Paris *boîte* and a different version again in a Cairo bar, until you recognize it for what it is: an amusing legend that you pass on or leave alone. The trade is full of them and most are invented – we take the Mickey out of ourselves with tales of exotic spies.

But this one was about a woman called Halfmask, a beauty born of the Devil, too deadly for any man to touch. She wore a mask that covered only half her face, so that she could disguise herself by simply turning her head. And any man, the legend ran, would be a fool to take her to his bed, because she carried death between her legs.

Legends survive; their source is forgotten or sometimes never known. We touch wood to placate Pan, the god of the trees. To every legend a truth, though we seldom see it.

She turned to the mirror, getting a comb. She was right: the line of the dress was perfect. Nothing showed. She said:

'You thought it was something Freudian when you saw it. Envy. It isn't.' I could hear the electricity crackling in her hair as she used the comb. 'One day . . . one fine day I shall get the chance I need. I won't know who they are – they'll be the enemy. They will just be "they". The people who did that to him.'

I still said nothing. She'd wanted me for a listener.

'You weren't just a stand-in, Quill.'

She was still by the mirror when I came back from washing. I got into my clothes and before we opened the door we kissed, just our fingers touching, for what I knew was the last time. Then we went down to the street and she got into her car.

Through the window I said, 'There's a legend about you, did you know?'

She laughed softly, looking up at me. 'Is there? It must be incomplete. One day I'll write the ending. One fine day.'

The telephone rang just before dawn.

Pangsapa said: 'Please listen carefully, Mr Quiller.'

His tone was utterly calm. I said:

'If it's important, we should meet. It would be safer.'

Kuo was holed up and in no position to bug the line but we keep to the rules. A rule is a fail-safe mechanism.

'It is important,' said Pangsapa, 'but there is no time for us to meet. Listen, please. I have had some of my people at work constantly and one of them has just reported to me by telephone. Can you recognize the man I sent with you to the Gymnasium?'

The little Hindu.

'Yes.'

'He is waiting for you near the steps of the USOM in Phet Buri Road. Go there very quickly. Show yourself at that place. If he doesn't appear, telephone me at once.'

'And if he appears?'

'He will tell you.'

He rang off and I knew there was some thinking to be done but I could do it on the way there because there was no question of not going. Pangsapa had said all that was needed and the situation was clear enough: the Hindu was tagging someone and would have to move on if the quarry moved on. That would mean that he wouldn't be able to show up when I reached the spot. He would keep up the tag and phone Pangsapa the minute he had a chance and report his new position. Pangsapa would give me his new position when I phoned in myself.

We call it Musical Chairs and any number can play. When the quarry stops we all sit down and with any luck there'll be a telephone within reach. If not we go on playing till there is.

It was a ten-minute walk so I walked. Patrols were stopping every car including taxis and the calmness of Pangsapa's voice alone had said *hurry*.

Two patrols north of Lumpini but I saw them first and worked round them wasting two whole minutes but saving five while they checked my papers. It happened again at the crossing of Plern Chit and Raja Damri by the Erawan Hotel and another two minutes got lost but I was nearly home.

He was still behind me, working well, and I had to waste another minute flushing him, using the side-road past Telephone House. He was the one with the splay-footed walk and I'd seen him opposite the Pakchong just after she'd driven away: although she had been with me it was his shift and they weren't taking any chances. Good of them but I wanted to go alone where I was going because Pangsapa had sounded businesslike and we could be in action again.

Flushed him, checked the flush and found it stood up. Brain singing like a dynamo because the waiting might be over now and the waiting had been very uncomfortable, worse than could be admitted. 'The mission is still running,' Loman had told me but all it meant was marking time and listening to the helicopters over the river and watching the patrols checking the fountain pump-house and stopping cars while the subconscious kept up its rotten little signals: *You fell for a decoy and watched them make the snatch and now you've lost him and he might not live. You used to be good. Getting old?*

A patrol-car turned down the street and I used shadow until it was past. Light was in the sky eastwards but the lamps still burned outside the USOM building.

I stood on the steps.

There was no traffic yet except for the police-cars. The trishaws were late coming on to the streets. The city had faltered in its rhythm and the day was beginning hesitantly.

Somewhere a helicopter throbbed in the low sky.

I was counting automatically and the second minute was up. Give it another, then phone.

Movement caught my eye. On the other side of the road was one of the tiny public gardens that form oases among the streets of Bangkok. The movement was being made by two hands. The head and shoulders of a man were framed by the leaves of the oleanders; he stood facing towards me; his opened hands moved slowly in a gesture that I should go to him.

For some reason he could not come to me and I checked the street with great care before I crossed into the gardens. They were silent. The sun was touching the first blooms and gilding a temple's dome beyond the magnolia trees. Dew was still dark on the leaves where there was shadow. He stood alone in the gardens, waiting for me. He was the Hindu. He spoke very softly.

'I could not move from here,' he told me, 'in case he went.' He was looking through a gap in the leaves and I saw the man beyond them in the street that made a right-angle with the one I had just crossed. The distance was some fifty yards and the gap in the leaves was no bigger than a spread hand but I recognized the man immediately.

He was one of the Kuo cell.

Chapter Twenty

THE SHROUD

The new day was fragile. It seemed to have dawned only here in the flowered garden. Beyond the garden the streets were still night-quiet.

Petals opened as the sun touched them; a branch of orchids hung above water where pond-lotuses widened their wax-white cups in the warmth. The scent of camellias grew heavy on the honeyed air and small sights, small sounds were coloured and sharp, alerting the senses as if they were significant: a bee hummed, a leaf fell, a bead of dew shone among shadows.

He moved again and I at once moved with him to keep him in sight through the gap of leaves. It was half an hour since I had sent the Hindu away. He had been glad to go, nor was I sorry: his fear of Kuo and anything to do with Kuo was distressing to be near and I was happier now that I was alone.

The Chinese moved back and I kept him in sight. He was waiting for someone and they were late and he was nervous because the patrols were everywhere. I could do nothing about that, only pray that a patrol wouldn't decide to question him and pick him up because then I would lose him and lose Kuo and the chance of reaching the Person.

It was the chance that made the new day fragile. I had a thread in my fingers, drawn fine, so fine that it seemed that the drop of a single leaf would break it.

If they picked him up they would take him for questioning and he wouldn't answer them. From some place – not from a ruin or a wharf or any place obviously to be searched – this one member of the Kuo cell had come into the open, purposefully.

Theory: Kuo was sending them out one by one to set up an escape route for himself and his prisoner. If they were left alone they would make contacts, extend the route more surely, protect it with strength in numbers. If they were picked up they would protect the route by their secrecy: the death-pill is proof against every method of interrogation known to man.

The chance was so fragile. I had to keep him in sight, move

when he moved, follow him and find his contacts and follow them through a city where police teemed and where police-action against any of these men would snap the thread and smash the whole day down.

Pangsapa knew. Whatever his reasons he was dedicated to tracing the Person and he knew that to put the police on to this man would be to kill the only chance we had.

The heat was coming. Haze was forming above the trees as the sun drew moisture from the green places in the city. Traffic was beginning, a soft rush sounding from the wider streets.

The man moved and I moved with him. He was standing with his head turned away from me and I looked beyond him and saw the car coming.

Contact.

The operation was already planned in my mind. It didn't follow that his contact would arrive on foot simply because he was himself on foot. I could have told the Hindu to bring me a car or send a taxi here to wait for me in case I wanted it but the situation was so delicate: the Chinese was living these minutes on his nerves and the unexplained appearance of a car might scare him enough to break his rendezvous and get clear.

He wasn't scared by the car that was coming because he knew about it and had been waiting for it and was already moving to the edge of the pavement as it slowed under quiet brakes. I watched it until it stopped, then took ten paces towards the entrance of the gardens and held myself ready.

It was a massive black Lincoln sedan: a seven-seater executive-style transport, flat-sided, with discreet steel fittings. The chauffeur was alone. He leaned nearer the Chinese and they spoke together and then the Chinese opened the rear door and climbed into the car and I did the only thing possible.

If I lost sight of them the fragile thread would snap and I might never see them again – the Chinese, Kuo, the Person. I had to follow them and the only transport I could use was theirs. The great Lincoln was gathering speed past the entrance of the gardens when I judged correctly and got the rear door open and lurched inside, pulling the door shut behind me as the chauffeur screwed his neck round and called something, slowing.

The Chinese told him: 'Keep driving.'

He was a young man, younger than Kuo but not unlike him,

136

slim-hipped and wide at the shoulder and with the calm eyes of a top athlete who has dedicated his life to challenge. His control of the situation was perfect. He had made successful contact and the nervous strain of waiting was over and his tone was as calm as his eyes.

'Be careful, please.'

The arm-rest between us was down and I looked at it. The barrel lay along it, a few inches from my liver.

The sole advantage of the spring-gun is silence. It is more silent than any powder-gun, however heavily baffled. At even medium range – six feet and over – it is inefficient if it has to fire through clothing. Even at four feet an overcoat will shield the body from most of the impact. The spring-gun can kill through light clothing at any range below two feet providing it can be aimed to strike a vital organ without hitting bone. As a useful weapon it has value only if its limitations are known and allowed for.

It would take its natural place among those weapons carried by a cell such as Kuo – a professional marksman – controlled. The sound of a gunshot in a city patrolled by massed police forces on the watch for anything even slightly unusual would provoke immediate alarm. The man beside me carried a spring-gun against the necessity of having to threaten or shoot while he was in the open and cut off from his base, and it was simply his good luck that this necessity had arisen in the confines of a closed car.

There would be another gun on him, for use in extreme circumstances and at longer range. At present the spring was the perfect weapon.

It was aimed well within killing-distance and the needle-point steel dart could pierce a vital organ the liver – without risk of hitting the bone of hip-joint or lower rib.

The Chinese spoke again to the driver in Mandarin with a Shanghai accent. 'Make for the Park and circle it.'

The Lincoln turned down Phayathai Road towards Rama IV. We had begun heading away from their base. That was inevitable. They would be embarrassed by having to look after a second prisoner at a time when they were desperate to move the first one to a safer place. My only hope had been to get the upper hand and either force them to reveal the location of their base or give them to the police after making sure they had no access to a death-pill. It was still my hope.

He asked me in good English: 'Where is the woman?'

The Lincoln had a bench-type front seat that was solid from pillar to pillar and immovable. The leather seat at my back was luxuriously cushioned and would indent up to a good six inches.

'At the safe-house,' I told him.

It was natural for them to think we were in the same group. They had seen us together in the streets when she had been tagging me. They had possibly seen us, singly, entering or leaving the British Embassy.

His immediate idea was two birds, one shot.

Six inches was sufficient. The barrel of the spring gun would be aimed past the front of my diaphragm by the time he fired.

'Where is the safe-house?' he asked me.

We were turning left along Rama IV and heading for Lumpini Park. The kite warehouse was nearer than the gem-shop and there would be more room to move about in there and a chance of doing some work on him.

'In Soi Narong 9,' I told him and took a breath and kicked hard at the front seat to jack-knife and press back into the cushion to give him the six-inch clearance that would send the steel dart wide as I brought my right hand down in a strong chop for his gun wrist.

'Be careful, please,' he said.

Blood began trickling from the edge of my hand.

There had been only a slight *phuttt* from the gun. Its barrel had swung up a degree to meet my hand and the dart had ripped flesh away.

A trained athlete reacts as fast as a cat, and muscle-obedience to the motor nerves is almost instantaneous.

He said to the chauffeur: 'Go to Soi Narong 9. Drive at a moderate speed.'

A police-car overtook us and the crew raked us with a long hard glance and the barrel bit into my side as a reminder and I sat still and watched the police-car slot in between us and the car ahead; then it pulled out and we lost it.

'What number, in Soi Narong 9?'

'The warehouse,' I told him.

He spoke again to the chauffeur.

Slowly, and looking at the Chinese, I moved my hand forward

so that the blood could drip on to the carpet instead of my trousers. He smiled, nodding.

When we reached the warehouse he asked: 'Which door do you use, please?'

'The one in the alley.'

He told the chauffeur to reverse the Lincoln as far as the first door. That was normal procedure because the alley was a dead-end and he had seen as much and wanted the car to be pointing in the right direction in case anything happened. It wasn't because he was nervous, and this fact worried me. He showed no emotion. At close quarters I like the adverse party to feel something, preferably fear, though hate is as useful. The category matters less than the degree: the stronger the emotion the more it will blur his thinking.

He showed none. That one word – 'please' – was an indication of his absolute confidence. He was a man typical of Kuo's choice: the brain and sinews of a cat, the heart of a machine.

The car stopped and I had three or four seconds to review the chances. They didn't look very good. With an ordinary thug I could have guaranteed success even though there were two of them because there was so little room to move: the Lincoln blocked the alley and both the door of the car and the door of the warehouse had to be opened and shut. Lack of the freedom to move is an asset when the adverse party is toad-slow to react. Fast reactions, such as I would get from this man, were dangerous at close quarters. This was why I had chosen to take him into the warehouse and avail myself of elbow-room, and why nothing could be done until we got inside.

The throb of the V-8 engine was loud in the narrow passage.

In Mandarin: 'When I have left the car, drive to the place. Tell them I will be there in an hour.' In English: 'Is the door locked?'

'Yes,' I said.

'You have the keys?'

'Yes.'

'Go in there. And be careful, please.'

They watched us come in – the big male *chulas* with their livid colouring, the female *pakpaos* with their slender tails. They hung motionless: the morning was airless and the opening of the door made no draught.

I heard him shut it behind us. The throb of the Lincoln rose and then died away. In the cavernous shed there were no echoes; his footsteps were muffled; their sound told me that he was backing away four paces, five. I knew why.

'Turn to face me, please.'

He had changed weapons. At five paces the spring-gun was ineffective. He held a ·38 automatic and it had a silencer.

'Silencer' is a misnomer. No gun can be made silent. A full baffle will absorb a lot of noise but it will also cost a lot of impact and can make the difference between a kill and a maiming wound – and a man with a maiming wound can run and can even fight and can even close in before the second shot comes. This was a half-baffle designed to cut down the noise without costing too much fire-power. It would be heard in a building or a street. It would make a noise in here but no one outside would hear it because the kites were themselves a massive silencer. Seeing them, and noting the acoustics as we came in, he had changed weapons with the instinctive judgement of a professional.

'Where is the woman?'

Sunshine fell from the skylights; we stood on our own shadows. At five paces I could do nothing: he would pump the stuff into me as I leapt for him. There was the chance only of selling him a reason for taking me out of here, for taking me to his base so that Kuo himself could question me.

'She's not here,' I said. Time was needed. I had to think of a reason to sell him.

'You told me she was here.' It was a flat statement, made without surprise. He looked around with small and precise jerks of his head, allowing me less than half the time I needed for a spring. 'But I cannot wait for her to come.' He faced me fully again. 'My orders are to kill you on sight if possible. It is possible. The same for the woman. But she is not here. I cannot wait for her.'

My spine had begun crawling. It wasn't a human-being inside that suit of clothes but a little killing-machine set ticking by a specialist: Kuo.

'They've got a plan,' I said. 'The police.'

It was the only reason I could sell him.

'The police?'

It was going to be difficult because he was a machine set for the kill and the ticking could not be stopped: a clock won't stop because you shout at it.

I felt the blood gathering at my fingertips, congealing as the flow became slower, like wax congealing on a candle. The wound was closing by infinite degrees; the body had set up the automatic process of healing itself. Given two weeks it would do it, even without medicaments. There was no point. It would not be given two minutes.

'They've got a plan ready for action,' I said. 'It will leave you absolutely no chance of getting out of the city, with or without your prisoner. I know the details of their plan. I helped them with it.'

He wasn't listening. With small jerks of his head he studied the area immediately around me. I said:

'When their plan is put into action, and Kuo is caught, he'll realize that I knew the details and could have told him in time. He'll realize that in killing me you allowed him to walk into the trap they have set. What will he do to you?'

The processes of my body congealed the blood to staunch the wound and preserve life. The processes of my brain worked to the same end. But I knew I had begun to die.

'Stand by the box, please.'

He jerked the gun, indicating the nearest of the long crates. It was to my left. He was a strong youth and could easily lift my dead weight into the crate, but why should he? One dislikes shifting garbage.

'In front of the box, please. At this end of the box.' The gun jerked again.

I said: 'I value my life, like most people. Take me to Kuo and I will guarantee his. And yours.'

'Quickly, please,' he said.

The sweat began and I was suddenly angry. It had always worked before: I'd thought my way or fought my way out of corners worse than this; there were scars on me but they were living tissue, that was what mattered.

Final appraisal of situation: if I didn't move over to the box he would shoot. If I moved over to it he would shoot. If I tried to go on talking he would shoot. If I leapt for him I would leap against the first bullet and the second and the third would go into me as I dropped. No go.

I turned my head and looked down at my coffin.

'Move, please,' he said and there was a slight shrillness in his tone. Not command. Worse: impatience.

One always thinks, if one thinks of it at all, that when it comes to the point there'll be a fighting chance or at least a dog's chance, however big the odds, and that one's mangy gods will at least allow that one is not led into the dark like a beast into the *abattoir*.

I moved over to the box, not in obedience but because it would prolong my life by a few seconds and in those few seconds something might happen that would allow a fighting chance, or at least a dog's chance.

Standing in front of the box, I looked at him. The anger had gone and my thoughts were clear and I was even interested in what he would do with my remains. He had allowed himself an hour to return to his base, so my remains must be concealed temporarily to prevent any alarm being raised. He would probably unhook one of the kites and lay it across the box, and go.

A bizarre enough shroud.

His hand moved fractionally into the killing-attitude, pressing the gun against his side to cushion the recoil.

He said: 'If you wish, you may close your eyes.'

I said: 'I thank you for your courtesy. I prefer to leave them open.'

'Very well.'

Because of the silencer the report of the gun was not very loud, though the fragile paper kites shivered to the vibration.

Chapter Twenty-One

THE NEGOTIATORS

There were three people in Room 6 with Loman and he got rid of them as soon as I came in but the telephone rang and he did a lot of listening, sometimes looking across at me without any expression.

Then he hung up and said tartly: 'I have been trying to contact you.'

'You got some news?'

'Yes.' He looked at my hand again. 'I have some news. What happened to you?'

'Nothing useful. Is it official, then? The swop?'

He went shut-faced and I got fed up with him because he never liked people knowing more than he did. I stuck one haunch on to the edge of the table and waited. He couldn't stop himself asking:

'How did you know it was an exchange?'

For snatch read abduction. For swop read exchange. Never a bloody spade. I said: 'Mil. 6 told me.'

'How did they know?'

'They've known all along.'

He stared at me brightly. He looked very polished this morning, like a balloon at bursting-point.

'They can't have,' he said flatly. 'They would have done something about it.'

'They heard there was a swop coming up but they didn't think the Person was in the running. They thought it was me.'

His small hands flew in the air. 'That is the *stupidity* of inter-Services rivalry! *They* knew there was an exchange coming up and *we* knew there was an attempt going to be made against the Person. If we had shared information we would have put two and two together and pulled off a joint mission. Why don't –'

'Christ,' I said, 'have we got time to reorganize Whitehall now? Just give me the news.' My day had begun badly and I didn't want it to go on like that. I didn't even know how I could face Pangsapa: he'd given me a chance in a million on a plate and I'd mucked it.

Loman spun a sheet of paper towards me across the table. 'Read that.'

There was no heading; it was just a plain type-written original hastily done.

Précis of Release No. 34/33/L202. Official approach made through Ambassadorial channels as follows. The Republic of China informs the UK that certain parties at present unidentified have offered to negotiate the immediate transfer of the Person to Chinese territory against payment of the sum of 80 million Hong Kong dollars. While the Republic of China has no interest in this offer it appreciates the grave anxiety felt by the United Kingdom over the situation in Bangkok and is willing to effect the safe release of the Person by such payment, given an undertaking that the UK will release a patriot of the Republic, by name Huang Hsiung Lee, at present under detention in Durham Prison, England, and will escort him to whatever place agreed upon so that proper exchange of the two parties can be made. The Republic of China would demand full reimbursement, at the same time, for the sum paid out. The offer is made as a gesture of amity among nations and in recognition of the inviolable rights of man.

Loman was watching me with impatience.

I said: 'So.'

He exploded with talk. 'The approach was made in the early hours of this morning and it is of course being given priority consideration. There is no question of declining the deal because no one can be sure of finding the Person before he is harmed or even killed. I am told that the exchange will in fact be made and that the arrangements are now being planned – in *parallel* with the intensive search currently mounted. It is thus a question of time. The exchange will take place within days from now; public anxiety in England is exerting enormous pressure on the situation – and the public will not be informed of the exchange until it has been effected, for obvious reasons.'

He was walking about and I stopped watching him. My hand was throbbing and I savoured the pain; it was the pain of a living body and I hadn't expected to feel such a thing again.

One more answer to one more question had come in: this thing *was* on government level although I had never thought it could be. China had it made. The snatch had been done by 'unidentified parties' – not by the Chinese. It had been done in Thailand – on territory that was not Chinese. It had been done for the simplest of motives: ransom. It was a motive quite unconnected with a Chinese agent under detention. But . . . as a gesture of amity among nations . . . and since there *was* in fact a Chinese agent under detention . . . why couldn't we all get together and live happily ever after?

Even commercially it was a neat set-up. China would pay Kuo 80 million Hong Kong dollars for the snatch and would get it back from the UK. Huang Hsiung Lee was being bought for nothing. Thrown in was an item of scientific data that would enable Communist China to build a weapon capable of challenging the whole world, East and West.

'A question of time,' said Loman again.

'How long, precisely?'

'We don't know yet. But the moment the Person is known to be on Chinese soil I am assured that the offer will be officially accepted. I am told that Huang Hsiung Lee has already been released from Durham and is on his way to London Airport. That will give you some idea how fast things are happening. I have been on the direct Embassy line to the Bureau twice in the last hour and the orders are specific: locate the Person and bring him to safety before the exchange can be made.'

The telephone had begun and he had the receiver to his ear before the second ring.

'Speaking.'

He jerked his head to me and I went over and took the line. Her voice was cool and slow and all she said was: 'I have a call for you.'

Now I would have to face it.

'Were you successful?' He didn't give his name.

'No.'

'What happened?'

'I lost the chance.'

We couldn't say anything much in case the line were bugged. He asked evenly:

'It was not the fault of our contact?' He meant the Hindu.

'No. He was very efficient. It was my own fault.'

Loman was staring at me and I looked away.

'It is difficult for you. They are desperate now. I hope for

145

further information. If I obtain it I shall need to pass it to you without any delay. Can you hold yourself immediately available?'

'Yes. Rely on that.'

'I shall do so.'

Someone was banging at the door and Loman went over to it as I put the receiver down. It was one of the Embassy staff and Loman spoke to him and turned back to me. 'Important?'

'Fishmonger.'

'Will it wait?'

'Yes.'

He nodded and went out. We had given Pangsapa that cover-name because of the tank with its blood-red water.

I was alone and wanted to pick up the phone again and ask her was she all right but there was no point. She was all right. All I really wanted was to hear her voice again, just because it was possible, as the pain in my hand was possible.

The police surgeon had put five stitches in and asked some questions but I told him I'd caught it in the lavatory seat and he'd shut up and got on with the job.

The strangeness had lingered because of the big paper kites and because of the close companionship to death in the final second: imagination had flared up. One of the kites had been directly behind the Chinese as he stood there with the gun held in the killing-attitude, and the kite was one of those with a face painted on it, so that I saw their three faces in succession.

. The face of the Chinese was impassive in the instant of the gun's firing, then it opened in surprise as he began falling. He fell slowly, and as he fell he revealed the second face, the face of the paper kite, fierce-eyed and cruelly fanged. She moved from the edge of the kite to watch him fall and her face, the third face, was squeezed in a grimace of loathing as she stood looking down. Then it cleared and she closed her eyes, and her face had the calm of a sleeping child.

The Chinese hadn't moved. Blood came from the hole in his neck. She had shot for the third vertebra in the cervical region, smashing it and severing the nerves. It was a surgically accurate shot, consideration having been taken of the limitations of so small a gun.

The fumes rose from the little barrel, grey in the sunshine that fell from the skylights. She opened her eyes and I stepped over the body and took the gun from her. She wouldn't want it any more. This was her one fine day and the legend of Halfmask was ended.

We walked to the Embassy, taking our time. The Park was on our way and we walked slowly under the magnolias like lovers. I didn't speak because she had the trauma to deal with but she felt like talking and she talked about ordinary things.

'Lawson phoned me soon after dawn and said you'd flushed him near Telephone House, so we put out the usual alert. He went back to your hotel and Green was sent to cover Soi Suek 3. I took the warehouse. It was just the way things went – it could have been any permutation.'

She reached once for my hand, quickly and suddenly, and I felt the tremor shaking her. She had killed because of what they had done to Richard: I had given her the excuse, that was all. It would take time for her to justify and forget.

Her fingers moved and I let them free. She said:

'I saw the car backing up – the Lincoln – so I went in by another door in case there was something I could do.'

I knew that her group had the keys to the place: she had opened a door there before, the night she had tagged Loman.

'He would – ' She had to get a breath and have another go – 'He would have killed you, wouldn't he? Otherwise?'

'In the next half-second.'

Justify and forget.

'I don't mean – '

'I know,' I said.

'I'd have done it anyway, one day, for any reason. I'm glad it was you.'

The magnolias floated their leaves on a sky bluer than I had ever seen it; we walked through gold light. I said: 'I'm not complaining.'

She began laughing softly but it went on and turned strident and I said sharply, 'Cut that out'. She was all right after that and I put her into a cab and told the driver the British Embassy, and walked on to the Police Hospital a few blocks away to get the hand fixed up.

Loman came back in ten minutes and didn't say why he'd been called away: they like playing it big when they're in the field with the agent – 'I have been on the direct Embassy line to the Bureau twice in the last hour', that sort of thing.

'What did Fishmonger want?'

'Requests availability.'

'He is a *very* good man,' Loman said. 'Don't underestimate his resources as an informant.'

'Christ, I know that. He gave me a lead this morning and it could have been good – damned good.'

He stood absolutely still, listening.

'Well?'

'No go. I got myself cornered. One dead.'

He nodded. 'Do you need any smoke out?'

'No.' It was like that with Loman: just when you wondered how much longer you could stand him he said something nice. He should have stood on my face for losing a good lead when we were desperate for one.

He was half-way to the phone when I stopped him: 'I passed it to local SB from the hospital when I was waiting for them to fix my hand. Black Lincoln, Bangkok registered, number and everything, spring-gun dart lodged in the rear door, inside – if they ever get the chance to look for it.'

He asked me about directions, coming and going, so forth, and I told him the essentials. He didn't ask about the bump: providing I didn't need smoke out he was satisfied.

'Perhaps they can find it,' he said. 'There aren't many Lincolns. But they won't pass it to the Metropolitan for a general search – you know Special Branch sensitivities, the world over.' He turned away and asked: 'You didn't report the casualty?'

'No.' It is always left to the discretion of the intelligence director in the field whether a killing is reported or not. Circumstances vary. 'You mind holding off, Loman?'

'Reason?'

'There's some more to do in that area and I'd like it kept clear for a bit. Give it a few hours.'

He considered. 'Very well.'

He was playing me softly today because we looked like losing the mission and he didn't want to stack up any blame for wrong decisions. He was leaving things as much as possible to me: it was the only lesson he'd learned. I liked working alone and he knew he'd have to let me. But he still thought we were going to lose.

I looked at my watch. They'd had an hour and a half.

'I'll report as necessary.'

'If Pangsapa has anything for you . . . ?'

'He'll have to keep it till I report.'

'Have you a lead, Quiller?'

'Straight run or a dead-end, one or the other.'

There was nothing for him to do but give me the overall score. 'We have something like forty-eight hours,' he said. 'That is the period within which they can get Huang Hsiung Lee from Durham to London and by air to the Chinese frontier. The Kuo cell will know this. They will know that the deal is going to be accepted and that no one must waste any time in getting both parties to the exchange-point. Kuo will make an all-out attempt to leave Bangkok today or tomorrow.' He came with me as far as the door. 'The feeling in England is still one of shock and grave anxiety. The general public knows only that the Person is missing and in danger. That is of course still true. Among those few in Whitehall who know of the exchange offer there is an added anxiety – that the exchange will have to go through and that we shall hand over, with Lee, a weapon of awesome potential to a Communist State.'

I said: 'Forty-eight hours. You can do a lot in that time. But we'll want some luck. Christ, we'll want some luck.'

I took a cab there and got out near the warehouse and walked as far as the door in the alley. I didn't hope for much but it had to be tried. The Chinese had told the chauffeur that he would be back at base in an hour. Thirty minutes ago they would have begun to worry. It would take another thirty to convince them that he'd got fouled up somewhere. If they could stand the strain of not knowing, they'd forget him. I didn't think they could stand the strain in their present situation: they had to find out for certain that he hadn't been grabbed, that he wasn't being grilled by professional police interrogators after the potassium-cyanide pill had been forced out of his fingers in time. They had to know if they were still safe, that their base wasn't quietly being ringed around with police in depth at this precise minute.

They would have to pick a lock or break a door and I didn't know which door they'd go for so I'd have to be inside when they came. I didn't have a gun because there wouldn't be any necessity:

If they came at all they wouldn't even know I was here. The operation would begin when they left and tried to get back to base without my tagging them there.

If I could do *that* . . .

The alley was clear. I had gone the whole way round the warehouse, cat-eyed. Now I went in, using the keys and locking the door after me because that was how they'd expect to find it. Then I turned round.

The dead Chinese had gone.

I stood very still.

Small pool of blood still on the boards, darkening. Kites motionless. No sound.

The nerve-chill was creeping down my spine but I made myself stand and watch the big paper kites for two minutes. They were excellent cover because of sound-absorption but anyone taking a single step from behind any one of them would set it moving, however slightly.

They hung dead still.

Findings: chauffeur reported situation but Kuo had not waited, had been worried that Chinese was *alone* with adverse party even though in control. A man ordered here straight away to ensure security. Body found and removed.

I was a little too *bloody* late.

Very quiet in here. Five minutes to look around. A lot of self-anger, frustration, contempt churning up the stomach while I tried to think, tried to hope there was still a chance, that they still hadn't gone.

But they'd gone and I unlocked the door and went out and caught sight of sudden movement at the edge of the vision-field and plunged into a run that pitched me down a dozen yards from the door as the blast came and the fragments tore at my clothes and my ears were blocked by the explosion.

Chapter Twenty-Two

BAIT

Reaction time covers three phases: time required to sense the signal, to decide on the correct response, and to respond. Relevant factors: age, state of health, muscle-tone, fatigue, alcohol, caffeine, so forth. Greatest artificial influential factor: training (i.e. habit formation).

The typical reaction time of a jet pilot receiving a visual signal (unexpected approach of another aircraft) is 1·7 seconds, this total comprising: 0·9 seconds to sight, focus and evaluate visual signal, 0·5 seconds to reach decision (evasive action), and 0·3 seconds to respond (move controls). A period of intensive training by ground simulation (bombardment of spasmodic signals) will reduce the reaction time to less than half, and such training – even after a lapse of years – will continue to affect reduction to a smaller extent.

Stimuli in descending order of speed: sight, sound, touch, smell, taste.

In the fastest group (sight) another speed factor comes into play. A signal appearing in the twelve-o'clock sector of the vision field (at the top) will produce the fastest reaction. (One is quicker to move when something approaches from above – a falling rock – than from below – a leaping dog.)

It was to my advantage that when I came out of the warehouse into the alley the signal was visual and in the top sector: both fast-group stimuli. But my biggest advantage was in the residual effects of training. It was two years since my last refresher at the house in Norfolk known as the Box of Squibs but good habits were still operative. (They lob soot-bombs at you and top marks go to the cleanest face.)

The result was that my prone body was sliding face-down against the wall a fair distance from the burst when the thing went off, and that I finished up in the correct attitude pointing *away* from the explosion with my face protected and my legs together with the soles of my shoes acting as a shield.

The three phases went like this. (1) Sighting of signal and interpretation. A man on the roof opposite the warehouse was raising one arm and his hand looked big. Interpretation: the 'bigness' was probably a grenade. (2) Decision: evade the danger specifically relevant to an explosion. (It was a special *type* of decision, leading automatically to the next phase: response. The decision to avoid a *bullet* would lead to a different type of response, because a bullet could reach my body infinitely faster than a grenade.) (3) Response. In this case the response factor took far longer to operate than in the case of a pilot taking action to avoid another aircraft, because all he has to do is hit the controls. To respond to the threat of a grenade-burst the subconscious has to evaluate a mass of data: the angle of the thrower's arm, which governs the time-period from the beginning to the end of the throw; the size (and thus the weight) of the grenade – data which affects the time taken to throw it (the heavier the slower) and the degree of explosive force; the distance of the thrower to the intended point of impact; the height of the thrower above that point (gravity aiding momentum); and all factors pertaining, which include mass, inertia, trajectory, air resistance, so forth.

Response passes to action: the body moves. But it must know *how* to move. Data evaluated has advised that the thrower's hand will take something like one second to swing back, jerk forward and release the grenade, and that the grenade will take longer than one second (as long as 1·5) to travel to the intended impact-point, and will take a further second to fire and disintegrate (according to the type of mechanism). The response thus takes one of two almost opposite forms: with less than one second available for the evasive action the target will simply drop flat and try to swing his body away from the direction of the throw; but with more time available he will try to put distance between himself and the explosion.

The decision made for me by instinct was to respond according to the second form, but the responsibility of the instinct did not end there. I was to run, but must be in a prone position in the instant of the explosion. Instinctual commands to the motor-nerves were thus elaborate: I must run as fast and as far as possible but *allow time* for my body to drop flat and draw its legs together a millisecond before the grenade burst.

Three psychological factors were helpful: I was under the

influence of mixed emotions – shock at the discovery that the body of the Chinese had been removed, anger because I had arrived too late, and fear that it was a trap set for me. The nerves were therefore pre-stimulated and conditioned to fast action.

During the full period of three and a half seconds conscious thought was uninvolved. The instinctive animal processes took over complete control in a spontaneous attempt to protect the organism. It was successful.

The blast-wave ripped the jacket from my back and the fragments hammered into the soles of my shoes. Masonry flew into chips and fluted through the air. Something crashed down near my head and broke up. As the ear-drums were relieved from the sonic pressure of the explosion I heard the scream of sirens. Half a minute later there was the sound of running feet as police approached from one end of the alley.

I began slowly to get up, and they helped me.

Two hours later I telephoned the British Embassy and asked for Room 6 and got Loman.

'Look, I'm stuck in a private ward at the Police Hospital and they want to ask a lot of bloody questions. Get me out, will you?'

Slight pause. 'This road?'

'Yes. Do something soon. I'm fed up.'

He said he would come. It was less than five minutes' walk.

The surgeon had had me on the operating-table for fifty minutes: fragment lacerations left calf, both shoulders, back of skull; abrasions and contusions both knees, elbows, rib cage; stitches in left hand opened up. He was the same one who had fixed the hand this morning and I told him I'd fallen down a lift-shaft but this time he was annoyed and said the injuries weren't consistent. He reported 'wounds inflicted by explosion' and satisfied himself that the Special Branch knew about me.

They were on to me anyway because the incident had shaken everyone up and they thought it might be connected with the abduction crisis. Three of their people were round my bed when Loman came. I told him:

'I can't give them anything, Loman. A man slung an egg and then took off and that's all I know. For God's sake get them out of here so I can think.'

They understood English perfectly and didn't like it and Loman had to promise them a full statement as soon as I was fit enough to prepare one for them.

When we were alone I gave him a quick breakdown on the whole thing: Lincoln sedan, scene in warehouse, return to warehouse, body-snatch, grenade attempt. I didn't name Vinia but said it was someone who happened to be handy. He knew it must have been one of the Mil. 6 group but it was safe enough: rivalry and friction is rife between all hush services but there is a tacit law that I have never once seen flouted. Nobody sneaks.

Loman said conclusively: 'It was a trap.'

'Not quite. They got there first, that's all, and took away the body to make sure it gets proper burial – they're Chinese, remember. Then Kuo thought I might possibly show up there to see if *they* showed up there when the man was missed, so he sent someone along with orders to kill on sight.'

'Those orders,' Loman said, 'will remain in force. At a time when the Kuo cell is desperate to conceal its activities and leave the city, they alert the entire complex of police services in an attempt to kill you in the noisiest possible way, believing a grenade to be more certain than a bullet.' He stood looking down at me, brooding. 'They are quite determined on getting you, therefore, and when they realize they have failed they'll try again.'

I didn't want to talk any more because hearing wasn't back to normal and the room was tilting about a bit; they'd shot some dope into me in the operating-theatre. But it was important that Loman should know that he still had a useful agent in the field and I told him:

'Of course they'll try again. We can rely on that. This is our first real break – it's probably the only break we'll get before both candidates are taken to the exchange-point and we lose the mission. We've got to find them and the quickest way is to let them find me, so they can try again.' The whole room tilted and I heard Loman say something but I shut him up. 'Listen. Get me some clobber. I finished up in rags. You know my size. And fix me some transport, something fast, case I need it.' His bright eyes shone through darkening mist and I cursed the dope and said: 'You'll do that for me, Loman, won't you? Togs and a banger, soon as I come to. Only chance. Give the bastards some bait. Put me on the bloody hook and swing it. Listen, Loman, do what I – '

Blackout.

I slept for eight hours and it was night. It took me an hour to get into the new clothes Loman had sent in for me and to argue the toss with the hospital superintendent who didn't want to release me without a medical clearance from the surgeon, but I forced a personal responsibility quit-form out of him and signed it and left. Nine p.m.

The pain was coming back as the last of the dope drained out of my nerves and I was glad of it because it goaded me into resolve: they'd set up a decoy and taken me in; they'd done an all-time snatch under my nose; Pangsapa had given me a lead and I'd mucked it and they were still holed up and ready to make their break for the frontier. Now I had a chance and it was the only one I'd get and I would use it.

The streets were empty except for police. They wouldn't be much help because a marksman could pick me off as I went down the steps of the hospital if Kuo had set one up. There had to be risks. They'd try again. Loman knew it. I knew it. But if the risks didn't stack up too high there was a chance of exposing myself and surviving and getting a sight of them as they got clear. It was all we needed.

They knew the danger of that. The man on the roof knew he could get clear even if I survived the grenade, because even if he missed I wouldn't be in any condition to sight him and follow up. But they meant to finish me and they'd have to take chances because they wanted to do it before they left the city and they were in a hurry now.

I walked down the steps and into the red sector.

There was no one waiting for me. They hadn't expected me to leave so soon. They might not even know I was still alive. I would have to show them that I was. The bait had to be fresh.

The Embassy was five minutes away but it seemed a long walk because one of the fragments had pierced a shoe and bruised the foot and because every movement in the whole of the vision field had to be checked. I wanted the pain to go on, life to go on.

Five minutes for thinking. There were several reasons why they had suddenly decided to kill me. (1) They thought I might have learned something from the Chinese before he was killed and might try to use it for a solo operation without telling the police.

(2) They believed it now to be certain that they could get the Person out of the city and to the exchange-point; I was therefore no longer a reserve candidate and had become expendable, so that any danger I might offer must be taken care of. (3) Vengeance: the Chinese had been valued by the cell.

Question: Were they so determined to kill me that one of them would be ordered to stay behind for that purpose when the main cell left?

I reached the British Embassy and went up the steps. I don't like steps: they are placed at exits and entrances where a watch can be kept, and the target is raised and has no cover. I wanted to be shot at, not shot, and the fine distinction got on my nerves.

Loman wasn't at the Embassy but he'd left some keys for me and I went down to the street again and found the all-black hard-top E-type parked at the kerb a little way along. I had told Loman something fast and he had picked a black one to be inconspicuous, with a hardtop in case I rolled it. He was good about details like that.

Assume the adverse party knew that the grenade had only injured me and that the nearest emergency medical post from the warehouse was the Police Hospital. They would look for me in three places: the Police Hospital, the British Embassy and the Pakchong Hotel. First two places negative.

I drove to the Pakchong Hotel.

And they tried again.

Chapter Twenty-Three

BREAKOUT

The Pakchong had taken on the chimerical quality of a Fellini film: people appeared from the shadows bearing candles, their faces floating in the light and vanishing as they turned away; gold leaf glimmered along fluted columns supporting invisible skies; voices piped through the gloom.

The concierge wreathed me in garlands of apologies: the mains had fused but there were electricians already at work. The lift was inoperative but a page would of course escort me, lighting the way to my room. I said it was not necessary and took the proffered candle on a dish, going up by the stairs. More candles burned along the passages in bowls and basins on the floor, and my shadows leapt on me and sprang away as I passed them.

There was one of the usual Aaraburi rugs in the alcove near the stairhead and I rolled it into ten or twelve thicknesses and held it in front of me as a shield before I kicked the door of my room wide open and went in.

Five shots rapid succession, heavily silenced.

At each shot I crumpled lower and brought the rug higher because the face always feels so vulnerable and you know the surgeon will have more room to work in the gross flaccid organs of the body if he can get at you in time.

But it's not pleasant even with some kind of shield: a bullet has a lot of force behind it and your stomach shrinks and feels knot-hard until it's over.

The vague form had gone from the window by the time I was on the floor but I gave him a few seconds and lay there with the sweat breaking out and the fibrous smell of the rug against my face. The candle had gone out when it had fallen and the dish had made a crash on the mosaic.

It took half an hour to make sure I'd lost him: survey of balconies, adjoining rooms, fire-escape, street. Then I went into the bar and drank a Greek Metaxa brandy, ashamed at my weakness and then angry with my shame, flinging up excuses: my brain had pushed my body into almost certain gunfire when I'd

157

gone into that room because I never believe in a natural cause for a fused mains in any hotel where I'm staying; and the grenade wounds were still fresh enough to make the body cringe at the thought of further punishment.

The bloody thing got its own back now: it wanted to sleep, brandy or no, so I just telephoned Loman and found him in and told him there'd been another party and then went upstairs again and dragged a blanket into the bathroom and locked the door. Went out like a light.

It was tricky the next day because they wanted to keep me under observation at the hospital when I showed up there to have the dressings changed, and it finished in a row. The medical staff themselves were all right because as far as they were concerned there was a bed waiting for me and if I chose to trot about the town and bust all the stitches it was up to me, but it was a police hospital and the police knew I was working on the snatch pitch and they were getting desperate for a lead: the warehouse area was still under hawk-like surveillance on the typical police principle of shutting the doors after the horse, etc.

The close-knit Saraburi rug had absorbed all five shots because the silencer had cut down the fire-power, and there was nothing to show on me. If the nurse had seen a new injury – especially bullet – she would have made a report and they'd have put me into a strait-jacket till Ramin came to grill me.

I had to send for Loman to help me with the row and he got me clear of the place. In the car outside he looked at me and said: 'How long are you going to keep this up?'

'Till they expose their location.'

'Or until you push the risk too far.'

'We haven't started yet.'

'I think I'm on the point of pulling you out.'

'For Christ's sake, Loman, you can't stop me now. It's our last chance.'

He went on watching me and I was fed up with it.

'I'm responsible for you, Quiller. You're nearing the stage when you'll no longer be in operational condition mentally or physically.'

He would *not* speak English and it annoyed me and I said: 'Listen, I know I look like a bit of dried shit on a doorstep but you can't expect me to look like anything else, you know that. Pull me out now and the mission goes right up the spout.'

It worried me because he had the authority to do it. He never liked his people to get into a red sector. Typical governess. I said: 'We're using me as the bait, aren't we? That's our policy. Don't start getting the wind up now that it looks like paying off.'

We went on for a bit and then I got rid of him by saying I was going to bed for a couple of hours at the hotel. He knew Mil. 6 was still on the job, watching the place, though I hadn't seen Vinia. If I saw her I would tell her to clear out. It was getting dangerous now.

Loman went back to the Embassy and I took the E-type to the Pakchong and left it round the back; the Kuo cell knew I had it but I didn't want to keep impressing it on their memory. Then I walked about in the area, and nothing happened, and I walked as far as the Embassy and back, giving them easy chances but not before checking and doubling so that if they missed I could try following up. Nothing happened.

After the grenade thing they'd found out fast enough that I was still alive: they'd sent a man to the Pakchong as soon as I'd left the hospital. Now they were being slow and it scared me because it looked as if they were concentrating on the final break-out and couldn't waste any more time on me.

Loman had said we had forty-eight hours and half that period had already gone. While I was wandering uselessly round Bangkok there was an aeroplane somewhere over the Near East land-mass heading for the Chinese frontier and Huang Hsiung Lee was sitting in it between two Special Service guards from London. The cable-lines would be crackling with coded signals detailing final arrangements for the exchange.

In the afternoon I decided to increase the risk. The main Kuo cell would be too busy setting up the break to spare more than one man to look after me. He might not be very good: a first-class marksman but not so good at tagging or static surveillance. He might have lost me a dozen times while he tried to set up a shot from a point safe enough to guarantee his getting away without alerting the police patrols.

A vehicle of known aspect provides a better image than a walking man. I got into the E-type and drove to the Embassy, leaving it right outside in the prohibited area behind the Ambassador's Humber Imperial and then coming out again after ten minutes, taking the steps a bit quick and checking doorways, windows, parked cars.

I was willing them to shoot and my nerves were sickening for death: I could hear the discharge and feel the bullet breaking through the flesh, could taste the blood in the mouth.

The street was innocent.

Down from Plern Chit into Vithayu and through to Lumpini southwards, driving slowly, checking the mirror, taking time at the lights in getting away, giving them a chance at every fifty yards. The mid-afternoon traffic was heavy along Rama IV and a jam was piling up near the Link Road. The sun's heat pressed down; its light shimmered across the façades of buildings.

The hum of engines was a soporific; my eyes were hypnotized by the wink of the sun on glass; exhaust-haze hung mauve along the street's canyon. The jam began clearing and I changed from first to second and kept to the slow lane and heard the faint tinkle of glass breaking somewhere near me, somewhere inside the car – something had flashed but I didn't know what – it wasn't a gun.

The animal brain was already at work, anxious for explanation. The forebrain went into the routine: check environment and note essentials. Then the body took control as the first fumes of the cyanide reached the lungs – the throat became blocked and the diaphragm contracted and I was fighting to keep the car in a straight line as the tears began blurring the vision and the lungs gasped for oxygen and the throat remained blocked because the brain knew there was no oxygen, no air, only a cockpit full of colourless cyanide gas – the quick one, the deadly one, C_2N_2, the one the Germans had chosen for the Jews because it was the most efficient.

Metal shrieked and someone called out and a front wheel bounced against the kerb and I had the door open as the handbrake dragged the treads along the tarmac, slewing the car to a stop.

Doubled up on the pavement blinded by tears, hands at the stomach, the first clean air sawing into the lungs through the inflamed throat and pushing out again . . . The smell of walnuts from the fumes still clinging to my clothes . . .

People gathering. Voices: *'Taken sick . . . Only the lamp-post . . . Telephone . . . A doctor . . . Going slowly . . . Nearly hit –'*

I lurched across the kerb and got between them and the open window of the car in case they went too close.

Even whispering was painful. 'All right now. Please go away. I'm better now. Go away.' The tears kept on streaming and I saw the people through them, their faces distorted, a woman pulling a child away, a man nodding encouragement as I straightened up. 'Please go away – I'm all right now.'

The air was dragged in, forced out, dragged in as the lungs hungered for it. The body could look after itself: it was the brain I was more concerned with, because we'd pulled off the trick, I knew where they were now, I knew where they were, we'd pulled off the bloody trick.

It took fifteen minutes to clear the cockpit, using the door as a slow fan, standing with my breath held and my eyes shut, moving away to breathe at intervals, coming back to proceed with the fanning until it was safe to get in.

The front wing had clipped the lamp-post and there were skid-marks but that was about all. The fragments of the glass bulb were in the foot-well. They had taken their chance, waiting for the traffic-jam to clear and then accelerating past, lobbing the gas-bomb through the open window on the other side and speed-ing up without a hope in hell of my following.

It didn't matter. The forebrain routine had been running automatically, checking environment and essentials. Three were significant: the driver of the Honda alongside had his head turned away from me; he had accelerated fast into the gap ahead; and the car had diplomatic plates.

Loman was wrong.

The Kuo cell had *not* set up an alternative plan for holding the Person immediately after the snatch. They had been confident of getting him clear of the city in the ambulance. When my call to Room 6 had stopped their run they had made for the only place available to them, the only place where they would be admitted without question and sheltered in absolute secrecy, the only place in Bangkok that stood on Chinese soil. The Chinese Embassy.

I drove there now, leaving the E-type at the top end of Soi Som Kit and walking into Phet Buri Road, going into the Maprao Bar and using the telephone. The time factor was critical now because they might think the gas-bomb had worked and if it were for some reason essential to kill me before they left the city they would make their break as soon as the Honda returned to base. It would now have done that.

I couldn't see the entrance of the Chinese Embassy from where I stood at the telephone but I was near enough to be on hand if anything happened. I didn't know what was likely to happen because it depended on Loman. I thought he would probably signal Ramin and get a cordon round the place. That was all right: it would take the pressure off me. Two of the grenade wounds had broken their stitches and my jacket was sticking to my shoulder-blade; the left hand felt tender and the cyanide had inflamed the throat. I'd located the Kuo base and the police could take it from there. The only thing that mattered was getting the Person to safety and stopping the exchange and it made no odds who did it.

The line to the British Embassy was engaged and I tried another one, watching the street, watching every face that passed, listening to the ringing-tone and the raised beat of my pulse in the eardrum.

The line opened and I asked for Room 6.

The late afternoon sun fell obliquely across the street and cast strong shadows opposite. A Chinese came into the bar and I checked him but he wasn't one of the cell. Embassy staff.

Vinia came on the line and my thoughts tripped fractionally as they always would whenever I heard her voice again.

'Loman,' I told her, 'Urgent.'

'He's talking to the Ambassador – shall I get him?'

'Please. Fast.'

I waited.

She wouldn't wear the gun again because the legend was ended. Her thigh would lose the disfiguring mark it had made and her mind would lose the disfiguring mark left by the memory of what they had done to him and the way they had done it.

You shouldn't think about anything but the mission, every day, hour, minute, second – because you can miss a trick if you even blink.

I nearly missed it but not quite.

I dropped the phone and threw a note on the bar and got out and walked fast but not too fast to where I'd parked the car – not too fast because if they'd left a cover he'd be on to me and

162

drop me with a shot because now they were serious and it was the break-out.

It was a black Rolls-Royce Silver Shadow that had passed the window and it was flying the British Embassy pennant at the wing-tip and there were only two things wrong with that: Cole-Verity's official vehicle was a Humber Imperial and the pennant would be flown only when he was riding in it. At this moment he was at the Embassy talking to Loman.

There was a series of one-way streets in the area and I had to go left and left again down Soi Chitlom and left again along Plern Chit Road, wanting to drive fast but having to think it out because the chances were that they'd be coming south down Asoke Lane – there wasn't an exit from Phet Buri to the north and they could only come south from it.

My hands were trembling on the thin rim of the wheel because this was an all-or-nothing run and I couldn't get to a telephone again without losing them.

If I found them.

I found them. They came south by Asoke and I was waiting for them in Plern Chit on the east side of the lights. They swung westwards and against the fierce clamour of the hunting-instinct I forced myself to wait until there were three other cars between us before I drew out and followed.

Chapter Twenty-Four

THE TRAP

Procedure remained well ordered for thirty minutes.

The Silver Shadow kept a steady medium pace within the 30–40 sector and for most of the time I managed to fit in a couple of cars between us. Nothing showed up permanently in the mirror. Two or three police patrols overtook us and the Shadow got a salute in passing. Kuo would be pleased by that. They had meant to use the Lincoln but when the grenade didn't work they decided to change the image. They were pushed for time and couldn't find a Humber Imperial and settled for the Rolls-Royce because it had a British enough profile and the Union Jack at the wingtip gave it the finishing touch.

The rear window was shallow and the glass was darkened so I couldn't see the people inside. Mental note: if it came to a showdown the Person could normally be relied on to pile in with a will, but he was probably being kept under mild sedation for that reason and would have to be counted out.

It was bound to be awkward when the time came to get him out of the Shadow because at the last minute Kuo could play his ace and use his prisoner as a hostage for his own protection. It might even be his plan to get through the Nontaburi road-block on those terms: with one small-calibre pistol held – *and seen to be held* – at the Person's head they could pass right through the thick of a machine-gun battery and dare the first man to shoot.

The only thing against that plan was that if Kuo shot his prisoner it would be his own suicide and he would die with his limbs torn off.

But I didn't like it and part of the sweat that was gathering on the rim of the wheel was because of these considerations. It was no ordinary prisoner riding in state out there ahead of me behind the dark glass window and to free him would be as chancy as picking the detonator out of a delayed-action bomb.

The traffic grew less thick as we cleared the suburbs because only those people with urgent business outside the city were prepared to suffer the delay in being cleared at the road-block north. The police patrols were less in evidence too: the sections between the city limits and the Nontaburi block had become a deserted no-man's land.

Situation at the end of the first half-hour: speed now a little higher, direction north along Route 5, almost no other traffic, sun lowering in the west to five or six diameters above the rice-field horizon. E-type: all readings normal, tank three-quarters full. Distance from Shadow three hundred yards.

A single knock vibrated through the bodywork and a chip of paint flew up into the slipstream from the nearside front wing and the shape in the mirror was identifiable as it closed up very fast and sat there at fifty feet. Honda.

The light was difficult because of windscreen reflection but a compilation of sightings gave me a solid image. Only one man in the Honda, Kuo.

Very sharp sound above my head to the left as the second shot pierced the hardtop twice and travelled on, leaving a hole an inch above the windscreen. I whipped down to third, second, foot on the floor, rear wheels power-spinning a fraction as I closed hard on the Rolls-Royce and evened off at thirty feet. Kuo would have to be more careful now to avoid hitting anyone in the leading car. He wanted to get his prisoner to the exchange-point alive.

I slid the driving-seat back a notch and my buttocks forward to bring my head low, sighting through the top arc of the wheel. The situation was bad now and I let myself admit it so that fear could alert the brain to survival-pitch. There was no point in overtaking the Shadow: it would expose me to a battery of five or six guns. I had to stay where I was, within the easy fifty yards' range of a top-flight professional marksman whose intention was to kill.

He was having to fire without sighting; in the mirror I saw his hand at the side of the windscreen with the gun steadied against the pillar. He had fired a third time when I had reached up to tilt the mirror to suit my new position but a bump in the road sent the shot wide. That was all right: he had time and he would have enough ammunition. He had seen the E-type somewhere along Plern Chit when I'd begun the tag and he had done as I had done, keeping two or three cars between us and waiting until he could close up on me out here in no-man's land where there were no more police patrols. He had moved in for the kill as a shark moves in when it is satisfied that there is no danger to be expected from the prey.

The rear window went snowy and the bullet came on with force enough to shatter the windscreen and I had to punch a hole through the opaque fragmentation so that I could see. The wind-pressure took the rest of it away and the small hailstorm struck my face and left me driving blind for some seconds. Then the rear window blew out to the air-rush and I could see the Honda again, filling the mirror. He had closed up.

I didn't change down for motor-assist because the exhaust-note would warn him; I just hit the brakes for maximum drag a degree below locking-point so that a skid wouldn't carry me on. The mirror went dark as the Honda came piling against the back of the E-type and his tyres howled as he used the brakes too late and smashed into me so hard that I was worried about the fuel-tank. Then he was smaller again in the mirror, rocking badly and then straightening and coming on, taking up his position again. No go.

There was nothing else I could do now. He would be ready the next time if I tried it again. I was inside a trap and moving with it at an easy 45 m.p.h. and there was no way out. A pale blur showed permanently in the darkened rear glass of the Shadow: they understood the situation and they were observing it closely. Even if the shunt trick had sent the Honda into an uncontrollable series of skids and turned it over it wouldn't have done much good because they would have pulled up and forced me to stop and they would have got out of the Shadow with their guns raking me in a crossfire. I had tried it only because Kuo might have been smashed up as the Honda overturned and it would have evened the score a bit before they finished me.

They weren't firing back at me from the Shadow because they could be certain of a killing hit and Kuo might not be ready when I smashed. They didn't want to involve him in a pile-up. In addition they knew they could rely on him to make the kill, and when he made it he would be ready to avoid the mess. They were working as a perfectly disciplined cell controlled by a pro-fessional of talent: only men like these could take possession of a man so great in rank that the free world flinched as it watched for the headlines in a score of languages.

There was no chance now for me to save him or to prevent the exchange. Action by the armed forces manning the road-block ahead of us might do it, though Kuo must have planned a fool-proof operation for getting through Nontaburi or there would have been no point in his making the breakout from Bangkok.

A sudden rattle of shot sounded from somewhere aft: he had changed to a bigger-calibre arm and was going for the tyres.

The sun was one diameter above the horizon and the sky was a sheet of amethyst and very beautiful. Herons flew up from the flatlands, startled by the crack of the gun.

The big Shadow rode along rock-steady. The air rushed against my face. The shape of the Honda sat squatly in the mirror. Numbness was coming into my body, into my brain. It would happen soon. So be it.

Sooner even than I had thought. In the mirror the gun flashed again and the sharp crack was echoed as a rear tyre burst and already I was fighting instinctively to keep on a straight course as the whole tyre broke up and jammed the wheel-rim and sent the E-type slewing badly without any hope of correction because the rim was ploughing into the tar macadam. No response from the steering: she ran on at an angle and set her own course.

The Honda was suddenly smaller in the mirror: Kuo was slowing to avoid the wreck when I smashed. The terrain to the right of the road was stony – a few small rocks and some timber and then a drop to the rice-fields. I tried for the last time to correct the course but it was no go so I cut the ignition and snapped the door-lock home and waited with my knees bent double and my feet braced against the facia board.

She hit the first rock and shuddered and hit the next and flicked over and there was thunderous sound as the first roll slung her against a timber pile. A lot of sound, a lot of pain, vision dis-orientated, partial blackout as the blood was piled to one side of the brain by centrifugal force, my voice shouting something against the shriek of metal on stone, then it was over and the world grew still.

Return to full consciousness was almost immediate. I could hear the low tyre-squeal of the two cars as they were braked to a halt on the road above.

Kuo would come down for me and use one final bullet so I found the window-gap and crawled through on to the warm soaked earth of the rice field because I wanted to die in the open

167

under the sky and not trapped in a metal coffin. It is most men's wish.

Pain was in total possession of my body but I kept my eyes open, lying on my side, watching them as they stood grouped at the top of the bank, their dark figures silhouetted against the strange green light of the sky. Then one of them began coming down and I knew it was Kuo.

Chapter Twenty-Five

THE FLARE

The scene was strange because of the green light in the sky, and I had to make a series of small tests to prove that I was fully conscious: a finger moved when I directed it, the eyes could close and open, my head was capable of movement. The greenness did not go.

The smell of petrol was sharp on the air; the tank of the E-type had burst. The fumes seared my throat and I breathed shallowly. I lay watching Kuo. He had turned and was calling to the group of men at the top of the bank. The Chinese dialect was unfamiliar to me but I thought he was talking about the green light, and he pronounced a name in the Thai tongue – Nontaburi. He was giving them orders of some kind.

They vanished from the skyline and I heard the Rolls-Royce starting up. Kuo came down alone and his face darkened slowly as the green light faded from the sky. He held the revolver loosely, confidently, but watched me as he came. I lay still and watched him back.

My brain was working by habit, just as the clock went on ticking inside the smashed E-type. I was aware that the pain would disallow the movement of my body unless there were extreme necessity: unless, by moving, there was a chance of perpetuating life. This wasn't conscious thought but the consciousness was aware of the findings.

Pure thought arrived at further information: Kuo was not yet ready to kill me, because he could have put an easy shot into me from the top of the bank, or ordered a fusillade from his men.

His shoes squelched across the flooded earth where the tender rice-shoots stood in little blades, taller than the level of my eye. He stopped and looked down at me, the gun held ready in case I moved. His body looked enormous, standing over me.

Surely there was no chance, but an old dog is full of old tricks and I lay without blinking, holding my breath and letting only a little air seep in and out of my lungs. Blood was still gathering

169

on me from the reopened wounds and a cheekbone had been skinned raw in the smash, and in the twilight I could pass for dead.

My heart beat, but he could not hear that. Only I could hear it, and feel the quiet ferocity of the body's ambition: that this heart should go on beating.

'Quiller.'

I had come to know this man so well but we had never spoken. He wanted to talk, but there could be nothing to say between us, because he had the gun.

He stooped over me suddenly, black against the sky.

'Can you hear me?' The accent was educated, authoritative. I lay without blinking, without breathing. His tone became hateful. Whether he spoke to the living or the dead he had to deliver himself of hate. 'Can you hear me, damn you? It was my brother you killed. Where they keep the kites. I want you to know. That was my brother.'

His voice shook and he spoke in his own tongue, cursing my spirit, saying the words softly like a prayer, saying them deliberately, reverently, ushering my shade into hell everlasting. Then he spat against my face and brought the gun up.

Pain shivered through me as I moved but I went on moving and the shot was deflected as I went for his wrist. Stooping above me and unprepared, his mind engaged with its hate for the thing that he thought was dead, he was easy to bring down and I worked on him with the strength of a madman. Reason was not totally absent: with one arm locked round his neck I was forcing his head down until his face touched the flooded earth on which we churned. I worked for a drowning.

He was a strong man but the dying are more desperate. His face went under the film of water and a shrill bubbling came; his legs kicked convulsively and his left hand scrabbled to reach the gun but I felt for the thumb and eased it back until it snapped and he screamed under the mud. Then I brought pressure to the neck-lock, freeing my other hand and feeling for the gun. His fingers were nerveless and I prised them away and jerked the gun clear. It splashed somewhere behind me.

As I fought him I sensed a strangeness in the struggle: when engaging an opponent one reckons instinctively the degree to which he will oppose. Kuo was young, strong, cruel, a man without pity, yet he was lacking in courage. There was strength in him but no effort, and I knew why. He was a Chinese and vulnerable – like all his race – to superstition, and when he had spoken to me in his own tongue he believed that he cursed the dead.

My sudden attack had seemed monstrous to him and the terror had withered him: it was not a man but a spirit that rose up against him and he was powerless. The process is not intellectual: small mammals are frozen by the same terror in the mere presence of a snake. So it was with Kuo the Mongolian.

His paralysis had passed within a few seconds: as a man of sophisticated action he realized what had happened; I had used the oldest of them all, the possum trick. But it was too late. The strength that had been bled away by terror within an instant would take minutes to return.

Sometimes he moved and violently, his legs kicking, his body twisting, his empty gun-hand crawling for purchase on me; but the lock I had on his neck was unbreakable. Sometimes his face came out of the mud and his lungs heaved for air, but he was choking now. Words came among the other sounds, at first in Chinese and then in English, and I listened to them.

He was asking me not to kill him.

Above us the last of the day's light was leaving the horizon. The young night was fragile, lit by the first stars, and very quiet. Mist came across the rice-fields and covered us.

Another spasm of choking shook him and the words started again, asking me not to kill him. I wasn't surprised: the deepest cowardice takes shelter behind the gun, and the gun was this man's trademark. Not that it is cowardly to wish for life; it is cowardly to beg for it. Wish for it, fight for it to the last breath, but when you know it's going let it go, don't beg like a dog.

I wrenched his neck again and forced his nose and mouth under the mud and kept him like that because I wanted to weaken him, or that was my excuse. They had screamed when the big car had gone into them and that sound was still louder to me than this frenzied bubbling.

Then I jerked his head up and waited till the choking was over, and gave him the edge of my uninjured hand at the side of the neck, a low-power chop to paralyse. It took a few minutes for him to rally, and by that time I was standing above him. I told him to get up, and we lurched together through the mud and crawled up the bank to the road where Pangsapa was standing.

His dark figure stood between two others; they were one pace behind him in the attitude of bodyguards. It was only when he spoke and I heard his lisp that I knew who it was.

'I was uncertain of what was happening, Mr Quiller, or I would have sent assistance.'

A big American car stood behind the Honda. It must have come up when Kuo was choking, or I would have heard it.

It was difficult for me to stand properly and blood showed through the mud that smothered me, so for pride's sake I said: 'It wasn't necessary.'

Kuo moved and Pangsapa said to the two men: 'Cover the Chinese.' Kuo stopped moving. His breath sounded slow and painful. Pangsapa said to me: 'Let us go back to the city, Mr Quiller.'

I straightened up and tried to stop the onset of giddiness. 'I'm going on to Nontaburi. The road-block. Stop them getting him through.'

'It is too late,' Pangsapa said.

'No. There's a chance.' As I began moving towards the Honda the first sounds came into the night from the north. Rifle fire, then machine-gun. Distance was a few miles, about where the road-block was.

'It is too late, Mr Quiller. I'll take you back to the city. You need medical attention.'

I stood staring northwards. There were flashes in the sky. Grenades.

Over my shoulder I said dully: 'Too late? Why?'

'Didn't you see the green light, ten minutes ago? The parachute-flare?'

'Yes, I saw it.'

'It meant that the attack on the road-block was about to begin. Sixty assault-troops of the Vietcong were flown in earlier today from the Laos battle area. In a few minutes resistance will have been overcome, and the Rolls-Royce will pass through. The aeroplane is waiting at a private field three miles beyond.'

172

There were no more flashes. A single machine-gun puckered the silence for a little time and then it stopped.

Vaguely I heard Pangsapa telling his men to take the Chinese into the car and guard him. Then he came up to me. 'You need to rest, Mr Quiller. There is nothing you can do now. The exchange will take place as arranged.'

Chapter Twenty-Six

THE RIDE

The guards arranged matters expertly and without troubling Pangsapa for orders. One drove, with Kuo beside him. The other sat on the tip-up behind the front seat, the muzzle of his gun just brushing Kuo's neck.

Pangsapa and I sat in the back. The tendency to drift off mentally had to be checked. It wasn't only fatigue and loss of blood: the road-block was down and the prisoner was through and that was that. The 9th Directive was wiped out.

But suddenly I was leaning forward and shouting at Kuo – it may have been only a croak but it felt like a shout, inside my skull – because I wanted to know *why* the mission was wiped out.

'*Kuo* – how did you know my set-up? How did you *know*?'

He was groggy and took a minute to answer.

'I ordered a microphone to be placed inside the rosewood buddha.'

I sat back, numbed. So they'd heard the lot. Got on to me from the moment I began searching the town for him, tagged me to Varaphan's, picked the lock and rigged the mike and heard the lot. And the two missions had begun merging, his and mine. One had succeeded. His.

I must have drifted off again, my brain shying from reflections on my gross stupidity. Pangsapa's voice was fading in and out –

'. . . but they said you had gone . . .'

My head lifted heavily. 'What?' I asked him.

He turned to look at me. 'You are fatigued, Mr Quiller. I will leave you in peace so that you can sleep.'

I hitched myself up on the seat. 'I'm not too bloody fatigued to talk. I was thinking of something else, that's all.'

He smiled in the pale backwash of the headlights. 'The English hate losing, don't they? It makes them so cross. I was just saying that the moment I had news that our friend here was making a run for it I called your Embassy in the hope of finding you. They said you had just been on the line to them, but that you had gone. Knowing your predilection for working alone I said nothing to them, but drove out myself along Route 5 in case there were something to be done. We were about to overtake the Honda when the shooting began, so we pulled back and awaited events.'

The big Chrysler flew smoothly along the deserted highway, the air-conditioner providing us with coolness to breathe. I found the switch and got a window open; I am not a goldfish. Sweet air rushed in.

'When did you know,' I asked Pangsapa, 'about the assault-troops?'

'Two days ago. But you know how it is with random information; I was told merely that a local commander of the Pathet Lao in the Communist-held area round Tha Khek had released sixty combat troops and ordered their transit into Thailand, under cover. I failed to connect it with your operation until I saw the green signal-light just now. I had wondered what plan Kuo had made for leaving the country and it was suddenly obvious. It's galling, isn't it, when one is faced with an event one should have anticipated long before?'

'Listen,' I said, 'what kind of plane have they got waiting?' I suddenly realized that we could get information direct. 'Kuo – what kind of plane?' He didn't answer and rage flared up in me faster than I have ever known it. 'Kuo,' I was leaning forward and my hand had the shape of a claw.

The driver turned his head an inch. 'He is only just conscious. Does Mr Pangsapa wish that we should stop and revive him?'

'No,' Pangsapa said, and touched my arm. 'You should control your disappointment, Mr Quiller. I have already dismissed my own, and it was as painful as yours.'

I let my hand fall and sat back. The adrenalin had nothing to do and it ran without purpose through my system and my pulse throbbed, flashing behind the eyes. I shut them, and heard Pangsapa lisping on.

'There is nothing more that we can do, you see. I am informed that the exchange is officially arranged to take place at the Laos frontier, on the Kemeraj Bridge across the Mekong River. The territory on the other side is in the hands of the Pathet Lao, which takes orders from Peking. Kemeraj is three hours' flight from here, so that the personage in the Rolls-Royce will reach there at ten o'clock tonight. He will then be placed under military guard until dawn tomorrow when the exchange will take place. You see how absurd it is to fret, Mr Quiller.'

'I'm human,' I said through my teeth.

'You are an Occidental. They are not philosophical. My chagrin is quite as sharp as yours. When you first came to me for information I saw reward in it. We settled for fifty thousand *baht*, if you remember. But when I began tapping my resources and learned that an abduction was planned, and not a simple assassination, I saw the opportunity of earning a reward of really immense proportion. You surely thought me impudent when I asked you to estimate your importance as an international agent. I wanted to know, you see, what your value was to the Republic of China. You gave me your estimate in the most appropriate terms when you named Abel and Lonsdale as a measure of your status. Both were agents, but they had more in common than that. They were agents who had been exchanged.' He had turned his head and was watching me. 'I thought you had divined my intentions, Mr Quiller, when you named *them*. But it was just a felicitous accident, wasn't it?'

So this was the measure of Pangsapa's fury at losing: he was taking it out on me. Well I wasn't going to show any bloody interest. I shut my eyes again.

'My intentions were from that moment clear in my mind, Mr Quiller. I would assist you with all my power to prevent the abduction and the exchange, without financial consideration. Unfortunately we were opposed by a specialist of high talent, and we lost.'

It was said with sudden impatience, and I knew he had no stomach for more. He couldn't take it out on me and remain detached. I felt a little better and opened my eyes and looked at his profile; it had the aspect of a sulky child.

I said: 'Did you have contacts? An agreement?'

'Oh yes. Through an intermediary at the Chinese Embassy. Kuo's price for the Person was £5 million. For you I asked half, and it was agreed. They were very confident that the deal would never be concluded; they were certain that the Person would be made available at the exchange-point – as indeed he has now been made. But it was an insurance for them: if Kuo could not offer them the Person, I would offer them you.'

That was why he'd brought the bodyguards along. If I had

got the Person out of Kuo's hands tonight, I would have walked straight into Pangsapa's. How much had the Mil. 6 group known? Vinia had said: '*If they can't get him to the frontier, they'll get you.*'

It was ridiculous.

'When did they promise to pay for me, Pangsapa?'

'On exchange.'

Something was getting trapped inside my chest. I said: 'That's rich. Two and a half million quid.' I turned to look at him. I was shaking now with the oddest kind of laughter and it came out in a series of jerks together with what I was saying. 'There wouldn't have been any exchange, you stupid bastard. You think England would hand over an all-time block-buster like that to the red-and-yellow bloody peril just to get *me* back?' There was something wrong with the laughter but I couldn't stop it. Tears were on my face. 'Two and a half million quid for one piddling little ferret up to his arse in mud?'

I couldn't say any more because of the shaking, but it stopped after a bit and left me as weak as a wet rag. I think I slept for a few God-sent minutes on the way into the city.

The Chrysler dropped me at the British Embassy. The place was ablaze with light and there was a mob of journalists milling round the police guard.

Kuo had pulled himself together and got out of the car without anyone's help. The man with the gun was ready to shepherd him into the building for me but I said I could cope.

I looked in at Pangsapa. 'Thanks for the ride.' It was a cheap enough *double entendre* but the best I could do.

A brace of police closed in on us because of the state we were in, and it took a minute to find my papers. Kuo never made a move. He probably knew that if he made a move I'd kill him. They took us through the mob and the flash-guns made me dizzy.

I walked Kuo in front of me all the way up to Room 6. No one was there and I told a scared-looking clerk to find Loman. He took his time coming; the whole place was buzzing with panic. When he saw us he didn't look shocked. He looked as if nothing could shock me now.

I said as clearly as I was able, 'This is Kuo. All I could salvage.'

Loman just nodded and went across to the telephone while I leaned against the door. Kuo didn't look at either of us. He was very pale. His hand had swollen a lot because of the broken thumb and he stood holding it. Loman was asking someone for a doctor and a police guard. When he rang off he came back to me and said:

'What happened at Nontaburi?'

Some garbled news had obviously trickled through. 'A bunch of Vietcong wiped out the road-block. Far as I know the Person's on a plane by now. Exchange-point's the Kemeraj Bridge, Laos frontier.'

He nodded. I hoped he would snub me for sending the mission down the drain, so I could shout at him. He didn't say anything.

'What's come up, Loman?'

I saw Kuo move an inch nearer one of the windows and told him to stand still, told him I was only waiting for an excuse.

Loman said: 'Huang Hsiung Lee was flown in half an hour ago. He's here now.'

'Here? In the building?'

'Yes. The Chargé d'Affaires will be taking him to the exchange-point at 02.00 hours. You are quite correct: it's to be the Kemeraj Bridge. Cole-Verity is making the final arrangements now with the Chinese Embassy.' He turned away and dug his hands into his pockets. I'd never seen him do that before; he probably didn't know he was doing it; but he couldn't have expressed his feelings more exactly. The show was over.

When the two officers came Loman told them who our prisoner was and they clapped a shackle on his wrists at once. It was then that I remembered there was a lot to do and I mustn't fall asleep on my feet.

'Loman, don't let them take him away.'

'We don't want him. If he could do anything he would have said so by now.'

Loman meant a telephone-call from Kuo to the Laos frontier ordering his cell to hold the Person on this side. Then we could have made our own swop. Kuo would do it all right, because he didn't want to die. He was for trial, conviction and the firing-squad because seventeen people had lost their lives when he had shot the driver and there'd be no chance of a life-sentence. But he couldn't telephone any orders to his cell because by tomorrow

178

they would have collected the sum agreed on: 80 million Hong Kong dollars. They'd take it and run, his share as well, the lion's share. There was nothing he could do on a telephone.

'I still want him kept here, Loman. In this room.' I got myself a bit straighter. 'I'm not as far gone as I look and I know what I'm saying and I know what I'm doing.'

He stared at me with that glassy look that meant he was going to be obstructive. He said:

'There is no point at all in keeping him here. He is wanted for murder by the Bangkok – '

'Oh for *God*'s sake shut up.' I lurched over to the two officers and spoke in rapid Thai: we wished to detain the prisoner for a short time and would guarantee his safe custody until we surrendered him formally to an escort of the Metropolitan Police in due course, Ambassadorial prerogative, British soil, so forth, but thank you for coming.

The one with superior rank said it would mean putting a cordon round the Embassy if the prisoner remained inside the building and I said that would be a very sensible thing to do.

They saluted with good grace and went away and a man came in before the door was shut and I asked Loman: 'Who the bloody hell's this?'

The man was English and had a black bag and gave me one straight look and said: 'Right, we shall need an ambulance straight away.'

'Christ,' I said, 'don't *you* start.' I went over and blocked the door again because Kuo was fully alert and handcuffs don't stop a man running.

Loman was looking inquisitive. He'd lost face in front of the police officers but he knew that even a guttersnipe like me wouldn't have done that unless there were a good reason. I told him slowly:

'Listen. There's a thing I've got to work out. I've only just thought of it. Give me a bit of time. I can't do it without you – without your authority. And there's some things I need.' His bright stare was hypnotic and I had to look down. There was a messy little patch of blood drying on the floor where I'd been standing before. I heard the doctor fiddling about in his bag so I told him: 'I don't want any dope. Local anaesthetic if you like. All I want's a good wash.'

Loman was still waiting and I made an effort and got my head up again to look at him. 'Get some kind of a guard in here. Ask Mil. 6 – those two bright lads, Green and someone – tell them to bring in some guns, that bastard's tricky.' My voice sounded tired and I had to make Loman understand so I got some more force into it: '*Don't lose him for me, Loman, don't lose him.*'

The doctor was trying to ease my jacket off and I had to stop him.

'Wait till the guards come, there's a good chap.'

Because you're helpless for a minute with your jacket half off and Kuo was watching me, waiting for me to pass out.

Then Loman told me: 'All right, stop worrying.' And I saw the little black Walther in his hand pointing at Kuo.

'That's it,' I said, 'that's the stuff.' The doctor started again, getting the jacket off, and bits of half-dried mud pattered on to the floor. 'What time is it, Loman? What's the time?'

He brought his wrist up close to his line of vision and only flicked a glance away from Kuo and back. 'It's 21.05.'

I said: 'Taking Lee out of here, two in the morning?'

'Yes.'

The doctor said impatiently: 'I shall need the assistance of a nurse, and some equipment.' He'd got a better look at me with the jacket off.

'*Loman,*' I said urgently because my legs were trying to go. 'I'll have time to sleep, few hours. Don't let me down, will you? Look after things. No dope – no injections. Wake me at midnight.'

The doctor asked if someone could send some blankets in for putting on the table, hot water, things like that, and Loman said he would see to it. I heard him on the phone and my eyes came open with a jerk but he still had the gun on Kuo.

I was in a chair and there were scissors at work on my shirt. 'Loman, you listening?'

'Yes.'

'Sometime before midnight, get it for me from the warehouse. You know where it is. The Husqvarna. Need it. You do that for me?'

'Yes.' He said something more but it all went fuzzy.

Chapter Twenty-Seven

DAWN

At 02.00 hours the next morning the police helped us across the pavement to the car in a storm of photoflash. There was no actual cordon because Loman had spent a lot of time with Cole-Verity and it was decided that the Thai Home Office should be told what was on. We now had permission to hold on to Kuo and to escort him out of the city.

We had him in the car with us; I had insisted on that. His broken thumb had been seen to and his clothes – like mine – had been given a brushing; they were crumpled and patches of dried mud still remained but we didn't look too bad.

After Loman had woken me I had privately told him the set-up. He didn't like it. He said it was a hundred to one against and there were risks. I said it was all we could do and if there were *anything* we could do we had to do it.

I hadn't said anything yet to Kuo because I wanted to spring it cold at the last minute so that he would have no time to think beyond the simple terms of the proposal: life or death. He hadn't spoken once, except to thank the doctor. That was all right: it meant that he knew there was no get-out for him; otherwise he would have talked hard, putting up some kind of an offer. There was nothing he could offer us.

The Humber Imperial was full: the Chargé d'Affaires, Third Secretary, Loman, Kuo, one armed guard and myself. The police car behind us was bringing Huang Hsiung Lee. I had seen him for a few minutes. Young, ascetic, dedicated, a lot of assurance: they might not have told him much but he knew he was up for a swop.

Soon after they'd woken me Loman had said:

'We've had a call come through. The Person landed on the other side of the frontier ninety minutes ago. He is being held ready for the exchange.'

'Thank God for that.'

Loman had said icily: 'I don't quite follow.'

'He's still alive, isn't he? I had been worrying about the

181

Nontaburi road-block action: there'd been a lot of stuff flying about and the Rolls-Royce crew might have panicked and tried to push through too early.

All the way to the airport Kuo sat facing me on the tip-up seat. Sometimes he looked at me but there was no particular expression. He had the eyes of a nocturnal animal, the pupils large and black in the gloom. I had no feeling of being watched by anything human.

There was a Thai Air Force transport waiting for us at Don Muang and by 03.00 hours we were airborne and heading east to the Laos frontier.

At Kemaraj the Mekong River is wide and the new bridge is substantial, tarmac-surfaced and with two traffic lanes. It was closed after the Vietcong had overrun the area on the Laos side and military posts were established at each end.

We reached the bridge just before dawn in a small Army convoy. The post was normally manned by a unit of Thai guards a dozen strong but today a special detachment had been ordered up from the military base near Ku-Chi-Narai, and immediately we arrived the commander reported to our Chargé d'Affaires: he was to lend us all assistance in the event of difficulty, short of firing into Laotian territory on the far side of the bridge.

I wanted to look at things so I walked a little way from the car. It was very quiet. There were upwards of a hundred armed troops standing at readiness here in the half-dark; there would be as many on the other side; but it was quiet. A man coughed, a light flicked on and went out, metal made a ringing sound instantly silenced, and the quiet remained. It was the battlefield hush of the hour before attack.

In the stillness I could hear the mosquitoes whining in the glare of the lamps above my head. Beyond the lamps the sky was black but in the east a crack of light showed. My watch said six.

Loman had not let me down. Walking was painful; it meant he hadn't allowed the doctor to dope me even with one aspirin. My head felt clear, with the super-awareness that comes from not eating. I was unhopeful; Loman's estimation of the odds seemed about right.

The new day came into the sky quickly and a car was started up at the far end of the bridge and there were commands.

I went back to the military convoy and got into the camouflaged saloon where the guards had Kuo. The dawn light showed his face to be pale. He watched me steadily. I ordered the guards out of the car. Only a few of us knew what was going to happen: Loman, the Chargé d'Affaires, the two Mil. 6 people. It was going to be tricky and we didn't want anyone else to know, especially the soldiers. One man, unnerved, might fire by accident and trigger wholesale bloodshed.

I had to bring the Person safely across to us without a shot. And send Lee back to Durham Prison.

'Kuo,' I said carefully, 'you understand English perfectly, I think?'

'Yes.' His fear was revealed even in that one word: it came out on a breath. His fear was all I gambled on – his fear of dying. That was why I had not killed him in the rice-field. No weapon is so powerful as fear in the enemy.

'Then answer my questions. Was the proposal made direct to you from Peking? The proposal to abduct the English dignitary?'

'Yes.' There was no hesitation. He was in my hand.

'What precise powers were you given over the military – Chinese and Vietcong – to help you mount the operation?'

'I do not quite understand.'

He watched me the whole time in the growing light that came into the car. We sat so close that I could hear his breathing, and feel his fear.

'For instance, you engineered the assault on the Nontaburi road-block by signalling Peking from your Embassy. Is that right?'

'Yes. I was able to do that because Peking offered me facilities before I crossed into Thailand. I did not use them before the assault operation.'

'And have you papers giving you any kind of temporary authority over the military in general?'

He produced two guard-passes and a special letter countersigned by the Commander-in-Chief of the Vietcong forces in Laos. I read this slowly, asking him for a translation of the words I didn't understand. The letter gave him access to the operational chiefs-of-staff of whatever area in which he found himself, and power to request armed assistance in strength according to the situation. It looked official and was obviously genuine but I didn't like its vagueness. I gave it back to him with the two passes.

'It should suffice.' I had to encourage him; it wasn't the time for doubts. 'Now listen to me carefully. You will have to make a choice. One alternative is that you are taken back to face your trial in Bangkok. You are certain to be convicted and executed. Perhaps you know the method of execution in this country. The religion is Buddhism, which is against the taking of life. The condemned man is therefore put behind a sheet of fabric on which a target is painted. The squad fires at the target, not at the man. But you will die just the same, and it seems a fitting death for a marksman.'

I watched his eyes and I was satisfied. 'The other alternative is that you walk to the middle of that bridge out there and make it understood to the Chinese officer in charge of the exchange that you are replacing the agent Lee. *You* are the candidate to be exchanged for the English dignitary.'

There were engines being started up outside the guardpost. A party of soldiers went past the windows of the car. The lamps across the bridge had gone out and it was full daylight.

Kuo said in a breath: 'They will not agree.'

I turned back to face him. 'That is up to you. You can use your papers. Tell them you have received instructions from Peking at the last moment. Or tell them that you have spoken to Huang Hsiung Lee and that he wishes to return to England because he is about to gain certain information far more vital than the information he has now. Tell them that his memory is not sufficient to retain so many technicalities and that he has a chance of acquiring essential documentation from sources with a contact inside the prison: he urges you that if he is exchanged it will cost the Republic of China the loss of scientific data that he could otherwise obtain, given a few more months in England.'

I paused so that he could think, but he said almost at once: 'I could not convince them.'

I leaned nearer him and spoke quickly.

'Tell them what you like – lie, bluff, throw your weight about, threaten them in the name of the Commander-in-Chief of the Vietcong forces, General Kweiling, who has countersigned your written authority and will punish those who disobey. *Use any means you can.*' I paused again to give him time. 'The alternative is execution in Bangkok.'

He said nothing. His eyes were blank. Only the quickened breathing told me that he was hooked. And I knew what was in his mind.

I said to him: 'There is a white line painted on the roadway in the middle of the bridge. It is for the purpose of the exchange. You are to walk as far as that line. Then stop. The other side of that line is your freedom. This side you will die. The other side you will live. You may cross that line only if the Englishman is allowed to come over to us unharmed.'

A klaxon sounded. A Jeep drove past. The first rays of the sun touched the wall of the guardpost.

'Yes,' Kuo said, nodding quickly. 'Yes. I will try to do this.' He breathed as if he had been running.

I got out of the car at once. The police officer was waiting for me and I took the Husqvarna from him. When they brought Kuo out I let him watch as I hit a full magazine into the chamber and flicked the bolt and set the catch to 'fire'.

'Kuo,' I said. 'The people of Bangkok are in mourning for those you murdered. Your execution would ease their grief, since it would avenge the dead. I was given permission to bring you here, and it is unthinkable that I should allow you to escape across the line if you fail to bring about the exchange. If they insist on our sending the agent Lee, you will be brought back and will return to Bangkok.'

He could not look away from the Husqvarna. Better than most men he recognized its terrible power.

'And if you make any unexpected move, if you run for cover, if you cross that line before you see the signal I shall give you, I shall shoot you dead.'

His head swung up at last and he looked into my eyes, and saw in them what I knew was there: my readiness to kill.

The klaxon sounded again from the far end of the bridge. I could hear someone talking on the telephone in the guardpost. Loman was coming across to me.

Kuo said to me in slow strained accents: 'What signal will you give?'

'I will lower the gun.'

185

They took him away.

Loman spoke to me before I followed the others.

'Does he agree to make the attempt?'

'He wants to live, doesn't he?'

I had taken up my position half-way from the guardpost to the middle of the bridge. There was a low plinth and I had pulled myself up to stand on it, using one of the iron stanchions as a support for the Husqvarna. The effort of climbing had opened the left shoulder-wound and the pain burned there. It wouldn't affect my aim.

Our party had been given orders to keep at a short distance from Kuo so that I would have an unobstructed line of fire. When he reached the white line he looked back once, and it was then that I put my eye to the telescopic lens. The range was close and he was looking straight into the gun. Then he turned and began speaking to the Chinese commander of the exchange party.

Several military vehicles had driven to the middle of the bridge from each end, making a U-turn and lining up facing the way they had come. A few minutes ago some civilians had got out of the leading car and I saw the Person among them. He was bareheaded and wore no top-coat. He took the few paces to the white line with an easy deliberation, his hands clasped behind him.

With my finger clear of the trigger I swung the gun and sighted on him. Strain showed on his face. If he had slept during the past three nights it would have been with the help of the sedation. The memory of the incident in the Link Road was fresh in his mind, together with an anguish more personal: his family did not know, at this moment, whether he still lived.

His self-command was perfect, and I had never thought I would witness such a thing as this: a prisoner, in the midst of his alien captors, was impeccably performing the highest duty of ambassadorship, which is to inspire respect for the country he represents.

I could no longer see him. The Bausch and Lomb Balvar 5 was centred again on the figure of the Mongolian and my finger was hooked at the trigger. Kuo was still speaking to the officer, showing him his papers, slapping them with his spread hand, his squat body jerking as he insisted on his authority.

His feet did not move. He stood within inches of the white line. The officer moved about, conferring with a civilian, coming back to face Kuo. But Kuo did not move. One pace would take him across this miniature frontier and into the protection of armed men of his own race, but he knew that the range was less than sixty yards and that the cross-hairs were focused on the centre of his back.

The stillness had come into the morning again. The groups of the exchange-party on each side of the line stood motionless, watching. Behind them at each end of the bridge the military were drawn up, their rifles at the alert.

I began to sweat. The big Husqvarna grew heavy at the butt. The cross-hairs moved by a centimetre across the target and I moved them back. I was losing the sensation of time.

A hundred to one against, Loman had said. The odds looked longer now, Kuo was still talking: I could hear his shrill voice and some of the words. They were to the effect that a soldier of the Chinese Republic was not expected to concern himself with the high and secret affairs of State but to obey orders. Any breach of this sacred duty would be signalled at once to his commander-in-chief.

The officer replied briefly and then I saw Kuo's hand flash in the air and strike him across the face.

There was a shout and a rattle of rifle-bolts from the military escort.

The scene froze into stillness, silence.

My pulse began hammering. This was what Loman had meant when he said there was a risk. Two hundred armed men faced each other across the bridge and between them stood the Person.

My left eyelid began flickering and I cursed the weakness in the nerves. The big gun was very heavy now and the cross-hairs were shifting again across the spine of the man in the lens. Sweat was coming out on to my hand, on to the trigger-finger.

The officer had turned away and the civilian was talking to Kuo. His accent was clear but strange to me; he was saying something about responsibility. Kuo nodded vehemently. The civilian turned to the second-in-command of the military escort and spoke to him and got a punctilious salute.

A shouted order echoed among the girders of the bridge. The escort presented arms. The civilian spoke across the line to the

British Chargé d'Affaires. A word was addressed to the Person'

Then suddenly Kuo swung round and looked straight into the lens. The cross-hairs dipped and wavered but I kept them inside the target area. I could see nothing outside the frame of the lens but there was a lot of quiet movement going on now: people walking, the slam of a car door, engines starting up.

I kept the aim on the Mongolian. It wasn't over yet and I didn't trust him. My finger was growing cramped on the trigger and the left eyelid was worse and I couldn't stop the flickering. I had never known a gun to be so heavy.

A car drove past towards our end of the bridge and another followed. The tramp of a squad on the march. The sharpness of exhaust-gas in the air.

Kuo stood motionless, staring into the lens.

Footsteps neared me and I heard Loman call:

'It's all right, Quiller. We've got him.'

I lowered the gun.

On the way to the guardpost where everyone was gathered I took out the magazine and threw it over the bridge.

Adam Hall

'This is how the spy thriller should be written: foolproof plot, switchback-fast, every fact ringing right.'
The Times

'Adam Hall is Top Boy in the spy thriller class.'
Observer

THE TANGO BRIEFING
THE SINKIANG EXECUTIVE
THE SCORPION SIGNAL
THE MANDARIN CYPHER

FONTANA PAPERBACKS

Helen MacInnes

Born in Scotland, Helen MacInnes has lived in the USA since 1937. Her first book, *Above Suspicion*, was an immediate success and launched her on a spectacular writing career that has made her an international favourite.

'She is the queen of spy-writers.' *Sunday Express*

'She can hang up her cloak and dagger right there with Eric Ambler and Graham Greene.'

Newsweek

THE SNARE OF THE HUNTER
HORIZON
ABOVE SUSPICION
MESSAGE FROM MALAGA
REST AND BE THANKFUL
PRELUDE TO TERROR
NORTH FROM ROME
THE HIDDEN TARGET
I AND MY TRUE LOVE
THE VENETIAN AFFAIR
ASSIGNMENT IN BRITTANY
DECISION AT DELPHI
NEITHER FIVE NOR THREE
THE UNCONQUERABLE
CLOAK OF DARKNESS
RIDE A PALE HORSE

FONTANA PAPERBACKS

Eric Ambler

The world of espionage and counter-espionage of sudden violence and treacherous calm; of blackmailers, murderers, gun-runners – and none too virtuous heroes. This is the world of Eric Ambler.

'Unquestionably our best thriller writer.'
Graham Greene

'He is incapable of writing a dull paragraph.'
Sunday Times

'Eric Ambler is a master of his craft.'
Sunday Telegraph

THE DARK FRONTIER
THE INTERCOM CONSPIRACY
JOURNEY INTO FEAR
THE LEVANTER
PASSAGE OF ARMS
SEND NO MORE ROSES
DR FRIGO
JUDGEMENT ON DELTCHEV

and others

FONTANA PAPERBACKS

Fontana Paperbacks: Fiction

Fontana is a leading paperback publisher of both non-fiction, popular and academic, and fiction. Below are some recent fiction titles.

- ☐ THE ROSE STONE Teresa Crane £2.95
- ☐ THE DANCING MEN Duncan Kyle £2.50
- ☐ AN EXCESS OF LOVE Cathy Cash Spellman £3.50
- ☐ THE ANVIL CHORUS Shane Stevens £2.95
- ☐ A SONG TWICE OVER Brenda Jagger £3.50
- ☐ SHELL GAME Douglas Terman £2.95
- ☐ FAMILY TRUTHS Syrell Leahy £2.95
- ☐ ROUGH JUSTICE Jerry Oster £2.50
- ☐ ANOTHER DOOR OPENS Lee Mackenzie £2.25
- ☐ THE MONEY STONES Ian St James £2.95
- ☐ THE BAD AND THE BEAUTIFUL Vera Cowie £2.95
- ☐ RAMAGE'S CHALLENGE Dudley Pope £2.95
- ☐ THE ROAD TO UNDERFALL Mike Jefferies £2.95

You can buy Fontana paperbacks at your local bookshop or newsagent. Or you can order them from Fontana Paperbacks, Cash Sales Department, Box 29, Douglas, Isle of Man. Please send a cheque, postal or money order (not currency) worth the purchase price plus 22p per book for postage (maximum postage required is £3.00 for orders within the UK).

NAME (Block letters) _____

ADDRESS _____

_____

_____